Maraldia – City of Orph

Printed in the United States of America
ISBN: 978-1475204179

<u>Illustration Team</u>
Storyboards and Concepts - Brandi Watkins
Final Black & White Drawings - Dyann Callahan
Cover Watercolor - Dyann Callahan
Chapter Graphic - Eric Callahan

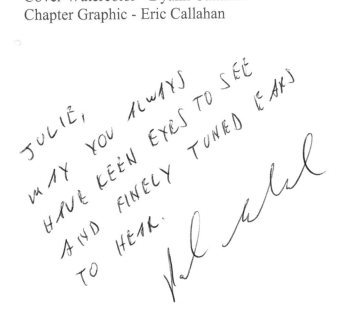

JULIE,
MAY YOU ALWAYS
HAVE KEEN EYES TO SEE
AND FINELY TUNED EARS
TO HEAR.

Acknowledgements

I'd like to thank a handful of people for helping this book to become a reality:

Jim and Mo, my fellow pilgrims who consistently encouraged me to get out of the cube.

The many people who helped edit and had the courage to offer constructive criticism of early versions.

John and Angela, for the use of their quiet northern retreat as a writing venue.

Dave, Nancy, and all the fine people of Esmeralda County, Nevada, for searching high and low to find me when I got lost in their lovely mountains.

My wife and best friend Renée, for being the greatest cheerleader a man could have.

My personal Rivoas, for providing a reason to write at all.

"I will not leave you as orphans, I will come to you."
John 14:18

Paul Schonschack

Preface

"Alas for those that never sing, but die with all their music in them!"
(Oliver Wendell Holmes Sr. – The Voiceless)

Anyone who has ever played a sport knows the feeling. The sudden realization, trailing your opponent late in the game, that if something does not change immediately the game will surely be lost. The realization that all your efforts and good intentions to achieve victory are about to end in defeat. This book is the result of such a realization, though in my case the stakes were higher than mere sport.

October 11th, 2011. Five old high school buddies headed out for the hike. We had been organizing hiking and skiing trips about every other year for quite some time. It's a great tradition to keep old friends in touch. That year we were visiting Jeff's older brother, David, and his wife, Nancy, in remote Dyer, Nevada. Our intention was to hike Boundary Peak, Nevada's tallest summit at about 13,000 feet and part of the Sierra Nevada range.

Now I'm talking remote. The population of Esmeralda County is about one person for every four square miles. By contrast, New York City boasts about 108,000 people in the same area.

We started to the trailhead early, before sunrise, intending to make the summit by 11:00 a.m. We planned to be down by early afternoon, happily backslapping and ridiculing one another like highschoolers do. The range had experienced an early snow which could complicate the climb, but we would not be at the top long so did not worry about it. Most of the climb would be without trails and involved scrambling up scree (loose rock) in a bowl section of the mountain. We were not experienced with this type of climb but it seemed simple enough, almost line-of-sight straight to the top.

Tip number one: Never underestimate the mountain. Scrambling up that scree for hours at the high altitude was no simple task for desk jockeys on the far side of middle age. Much of the climb was conducted on all fours as sections of the mountain grew steeper.

Tip number two: Never split up. Jeff and I, in our misguided zeal for glory, ended up getting ahead of Larry and Dennis (the fifth man, Tim, wisely stayed back at the ranch and watched through a telescope).

For me, the end result of violating the above two tips was that upon reaching the top at roughly 11:30 a.m., I had no idea where any of my fellow climbers were. I only knew that Jeff had already come and gone and Larry and Dennis had decided not to ascend the final peak (I had learned that fact via brief cell contact with Tim back at the ranch – only possible at the mountain ridges). I also knew that I was exhausted in knee deep snow and exposed to the whipping cold wind.

I began to feel a slight panic creep over me, born of my newly realized vulnerability at being alone at the top. I seriously wanted to get off the mountain and onto the backslapping part of that day's schedule. My intent was to reverse course, follow my snow tracks back to the rock outcropping at the lower ridge, and make a left down the mountain bowl.

Tip number three: Stop and look at the big picture, especially when it comes to major decisions.

A slippery decent that demanded serious attention on each step, combined with an urgency to get out of the wind coerced me into violating tip number three. I hurriedly followed the first tracks I saw, which in retrospect I believe to be Jeff's who had ascended from another ridge. I followed the tracks as quickly as possible in the wrong direction and, not finding Larry and

Dennis at what I thought was the original rock outcropping, made my left turn in search of them, plunging headlong off the wrong side of the mountain.

For years I've taken pride in keeping a cool head under pressure. Spock from the original Star Trek series was my hero. No emotion, just logic.

Forget it.

Spock would have paused initially at the incorrect rock outcropping to survey his situation when first having an inkling that something was askew. Instead, I frantically descended several hundred feet down steep terrain covered in deep snow shouting for Larry and Dennis, trying to convince myself that I was still on the right track and that they would be waiting over the next rise.

No such luck. Coming to the realization that I did not know where I was, and not having the strength to make it back to where I had been, I seized upon the first plausible option that presented itself. In the far distance, maybe eight miles ahead and a mile below, was a road. I thought it must be a major road if I could see it so well from such distance. The only thing standing between me and that road was the initial steep descent I was on, a trek through a lower canyon following the creek with fresh snowmelt, and an easy jaunt across a high desert valley to the road. I conceded that the boys would label me a chucklehead and agree that they should never let me out of their sight again, but that was nothing new and I willingly accepted my fate. I plunged with new vigor toward the canyon, aiming for the creek bed. It only took about 40 minutes to slide and tumble down that slope.

That is when I realized it was getting late in the game and I was down by a considerable amount. The creek bed which I had assumed to be easy going was impassable, grown thick with brush and thistles. The only way to make it through that canyon was going to be tracking along above the creek on the steep cliffs to either side. However, those cliffs were mutated versions of the scree fields I'd already encountered, and steeper. The only way to negotiate those inclines was to hop from one bit of sparse plant growth to the next and hope that it would hold my weight. Every misstep sent me sliding back toward the creek bed and ripped new holes in my quickly shredding pants. I realized this was going to be very slow going.

At such a time as this, when the outcome is in doubt and one possible scenario is dying in the wilderness, a man's thoughts turn to his family, right?

Right or wrong, mine did not. It turned to this book.

There is a story in the Bible about a rich man who invested differing amounts of money with three servants and went on a journey. The parable is about God's investment in us. Two of the servants obeyed the master, took some risk and made an increase of the investment left with them. The third hid the money in the ground due to fear, laziness, and disregard for the master's wishes. The first two servants were joyfully commended for their obedience and diligence at the master's return. The third? Well, not so joyful. (Matthew 25: 13-30)

Over the years various people have told me that I have a natural skill with words, and I've come to believe it to be an investment from God. I've never studied writing. For crying out loud, I've been an engineer for 28 years. Have you ever read anything written by an engineer? Maybe the assembly instructions to that barbeque with 1,000 pieces, the one that still had 50 pieces left when you finished? Then you know what I mean. In any case, with the encouragement of friends I nonchalantly started writing this book several years ago with an intention to finish it "someday" when I had the time. Not a great deal of urgency around it though; there is plenty of time, right?

Are you getting the picture? Servant number three stuck at the bottom of a steep canyon in one of the most remote parts of the planet, and I think I hear the Master coming. Maybe all of this is just bad theology on my part; an unnecessarily severe reading of the parable. Maybe, but if men can hear from God at all, and I think they can, it is the message I believe He spoke to me. I voiced my fears to the One who originally told the parable 2,000 years ago, refilled my camelback with fresh snowmelt, and started climbing.

It took 14 hours to traverse the next three miles, falling and stumbling countless times (I actually started counting at one point, but soon gave up). When the sun went down I could not see well enough to continue. I could barely pick my way through in the daylight and I knew if I hurt myself there was no way I could continue. I remembered hearing that there were cougars and bears in those mountains and wondered how much I might be able to do with my walking stick to protect myself during the night. I hunkered down in a fetal position next to a sheer canyon wall and covered myself with as much brush as possible for warmth. I was wet from tumbling through the snow and crisscrossing the freezing creek and the air was beginning to get cold. In addition I began detecting a rattling in my lungs, a result of spending too much time at an altitude my body was not used to. I shivered uncontrollably, dreading the next 10 hours until the sun again lit the canyon.

Then a literal ray of hope appeared. High on the canyon wall I began to see moonlight illuminate those austere formations. I wished I had paid more attention in high school astronomy and wondered if the trajectory of the moon would bring it into a position that would light this high and narrow sliver of a canyon. Within 15 minutes my question was answered. The light progressed down the far wall of the canyon and across the creek bed to my position. It was the one day of the month when the moon was at its full 100% brightness and it looked to me like daylight after an hour in the dark.

I got up, walking stick in hand, and started picking my way through the scree. I was awed by the moonlit beauty of that place and thanked the Master for the moon, taking it as a sign that the game was not over yet.

About nine hours later I cleared the canyon and was met with the relatively flat valley leading to the road a few easy miles distant. I began trying my cell phone again, whose dying battery I had been saving, but still no signal. Halfway to the road I caught a brief cell tower signal and made contact with the boys, telling them I did not know where I was but would contact them when I got to the road and figured it out.

Upon getting to the road, I found that not a single vehicle would stop for me. Looking back I can see why. Four thirty in the morning; crazed-looking man waving a big walking stick in the air; desolate road; entire back end of his pants ripped open. Pretty sure I would not have stopped either.

Turning west at the road was another life saver, given that the signs for the California/Nevada border were only half a mile distant and provided all the location information needed for the last text message to the boys before the cell battery went dead, and the tenuous cell tower signal faded out again.

Within the hour Nancy and Dave had called off the search and rescue teams from multiple counties which had been out late into the night and scooped me up from the far side of the mountain. The boys and I even made it back to Vegas for our scheduled flights that day.

So, with a renewed sense of purpose, here are my childish scribblings. My attempt to invest what the Master entrusted before He returns…or I return to Him.

Shooting to be servant number two,

Paul Schonschack

"...In the clefts of the rock, in the hiding places on the mountainside, show me your face, let me hear your voice." Song of Songs 2:14

Epilogue to Preface

On September 10, 2012, the boys and I undertook the same hike (dubbed "the redemption hike"), except this time a little wiser. I can happily report that we reached the summit, together. A proof copy of this book is buried there, facing west toward my moonlit canyon.

Author Bio and Book Dedication

Paul Schonschack graduated from Wayne State University in Detroit, Michigan, with a Bachelor of Science in Electrical Engineering. He has worked in automotive design and validation for almost 30 years. He is the youngest in a family of eight children, the 28 year husband of one lovely wife, and the father of four adult children. Paul and Renée Schonschack live in Farmington, Michigan, U.S.A.

Paul would enjoy hearing any feedback you have on this story. Comments can be emailed to maraldiacomment@gmail.com. Thanks!

All profits from the sale of this book, in any form, are being donated to Living Hope International (LHI). LHI is an orphanage in Zambia, Africa, committed to showing the adoptive love of God to orphans.

For more information on Living Hope International visit
http://www.livinghopeinternational.org/.

As Keeres turned the final corner of the city wall, a vicious snarling met his ears.

"Fffsssseeeeooooeeee!" he whistled as loud as he could, hoping to scare the beasts into retreat.

He had seen this scenario before, the wild grey wolves for whom the wall was built scenting out the new Maraldian young that were found each sunrise outside the city wall. The sad outcome was usually an infant torn to pieces by the hungry wolves. If it were not for the cadre of 30 watchers that scoured the 84 stanion (about 42 miles) of city wall each sunrise looking for the children, the Maraldian race would be no more.

"Fffsssseeeeooooeeee! HEY! HAH!" he whistled and shouted, spurring his mount into frenzied motion.

Plunging headlong and sword drawn, he knew the wolves could see him but the fangs would not be within range of his typical Maraldian nearsightedness until he was within 30 paces. While still a few seconds beyond his visual range, Keeres detected that the snarling had turned to yelping and he wondered if the wolves had set upon one another, fighting over the infant.

All the better, he thought, *perhaps I am not too late to save the child.*

"Get away from the child you wicked beasts!" Keeres did what he could to distract and confuse the wolves as he closed the distance. By the time they came into view the noise had abated.

Sweating and nerves taught, Keeres could not comprehend what his eyes now told him. No tussling animals or violent motion, no blur of action before his weak eyes.

~ 9 ~

"What in the name of the Givers is this?" he spoke aloud to himself.

He slowed to a cantor as he realized that speed was no longer of the essence. Dismounting and approaching the scene, he found not a torn child but six torn wolves, and a sleeping child in the midst.

Stunned and shaking Keeres collapsed to his knees in disbelief and wonder. *What manner of child must this be?*

His long suppressed desire for fatherhood now boiled over, "This one I reserve for Locenes," he vowed to the child and to himself.

His wife, Locenes, had dreamt only last week of a female child in their home and they were now nearing the top of the adoption list after many months of waiting.

"Waaah..eeeehheeh..waah!"

The stirring child forced his ponderings into action. He wrapped the infant girl in the fresh linens carried by each watcher.

"Oh, quiet now baby, Keeres has you. Will you sing a song with me?" Keeres hummed a Maraldian lullaby, soothing the child as it nestled under his chin and against his breast.

Keeres interrupted the lullaby to speak to the child, his voice equally soothing, "I will petition the council to move us up on the list. They know me to be a most faithful citizen, perhaps I can win their favor."

He was developing a plan, and before remounting for the ride back into the city, plunged his sword deep into the belly of a dead wolf.

"That ought to do it," he said to the child as he inspected the stained blade.

Before Keeres made the city entrance he was met by another watcher; a police lieutenant he had known for years.

"Yey ho! Brother Keeres! You have been the lucky one today I see!"

"Yes indeed, more than you know," Keeres replied and in whispered tones enlisting the friend in his scheme with instructions and backslaps, though he said not a thing of the mysterious wolf slayer.

As he made his way onto the city streets of flat puzzle fit stone, glinting in the new morning sun, he was greeted by the usual fanfare for any watcher finding a child.

"Yey ho! Well done Keeres!" applauded the fat grandmothers in their bright pleated dresses just assembling at the bakery for morning tea.

A salute from an off duty watcher, a nod from a new mother rocking her child behind a front room window, all looked on with approval.

"Yey ho!" Keeres replied to each in his usual bright manner.

Keeres was what some call a "friendly faced fellow," clean shaven, dark hair, with wide blue eyes and natural smiling curve to his mouth. He looked the part of one with whom men instinctively feel comfortable, and whom swindlers target as naïve (though Keeres was wilier than most).

"Yey ho! Keeres! What have we today? Boy or girl?" the plump waiting nursemaid inquired as Keeres approached the city nursery, the first home of all Maraldian children until the adopted parents could be summoned. Though all Maraldians were familiar with "natural" birth in the animal kingdom, they readily (though mixed with a degree of wonder) accepted their own more mystical beginnings at the city wall.

"Yey ho!" returned Keeres with a wave as he trotted on by.

Her broad smile turning to shock, "Keeres! Where are you going? Bring that child here at once! This is no time for foolishness!" she scolded and shook her finger and pulled up the layers of her long pleated skirts to take a quick step in his direction.

Keeres picked up his pace a bit at her entreaty and glanced back to see her dart inside the nursery for help. He trotted as quickly as he dared through neighborhoods of two story houses, back-to-back stone built clusters of four, alleyways between each cluster. He knew he would soon have pursuers. A few moments later he was at the Maraldian Capitol building.

"Well well, to what do we owe the honor of this unscheduled visit, friend Keeres?" Lered, the short and stout council chair, welcomed as Keeres carefully dismounted with the child at the Capitol steps. He was eyeing the child and suspected something unusual.

Keeres spoke, looking over his shoulder for the angry nursemaid, "May we go inside?"

It was fortunate for Keeres that the city leaders had already been assembled that morning for a matter which, at the last moment, resolved itself out of council.

"Lered, I beg you to allow me an audience with the council!" Keeres pleaded.

Lered brushed back light thinning hair with calloused hands, exposing the weathered lines of his face, "It would be highly unusual Keeres. Can you state your reasons for such urgency?"

"I wish to petition for adoption of today's child," was all Keeres would say.

Lered raised one eyebrow as he turned to make the arrangements, "Page boy, assemble the council." Lered made it clear that the good reputation of Keeres was at stake as he whispered, "It is not for anyone that I would do this Keeres. Your reputation serves you well, but do not embarrass me."

Keeres' scheme had worked so far and he gave a slight nod, "Thank you, Lered."

Keeres regarded Lered as an excellent council chair, as many in Maraldia did, in part because he was not from the normal circles of power typical for that position. In his early career he had gained high regard as one who would fairly settle disputes among his fellow farm hands. He often invited disputing parties to a game of henga and in the course of lighthearted play would resolve the contentious matter. Taking notice of these skills, his superiors offered him the position of city ombudsman and he eventually rose to the council chair.

"Please, keep the child safe for a few moments," Keeres said to the council clerk as he brushed his lips across the soft wispy hair of the infant and handed her over. Keeres composed himself as best he could in the waiting room to the council chambers.

"I should have worn my better tunic," he chided himself for his common appearance, tunic and loose breeches suited for labor.

"But my boots shall carry the day!" he joked with himself in an attempt to shake his nervousness.

He had always been a bit "boot strange" and he knew it, wearing those with outdated thick leather laces weaving round and round the leg, ankle to knee over his breeches. But he loved them and would change for none.

"This way," the clerk spoke softly and ushered Keeres into the council chambers.

Though frequently working around the courthouse couriering horses, Keeres had never actually been into the council chambers.

"Oh!" Keeres exclaimed softly as he entered through the chamber doors.

He was thrown aback to find himself a full floor below the elevated council seats, in the bottom of a bowl as it were. The half circle, in which these high back seats were arranged, along with the dark ornate wooden desks behind which they sat, made an effective barrier between the petitioner and the petitioned. Staircases to the left and right providing access to these elevated positions. A high circular domed ceiling complete with historical figures in relief all around added to the humbling effect upon those addressing the council.

"Please approach the petitioning table Keeres," Lered instructed.

A modest but lengthy table for those given an audience bisected the room.

Amidst these influences Keeres formulated his reasoning as to why he should come to the top of the list instead of waiting his turn, "Oh high council, rulers of our great city, I thank you for this hearing. Please bear my short petition with your usual grace and patience."

Keeres had heard that a certain measured flattery was a prerequisite to any successful petition.

"You will have our patience Keeres, only be direct with your reasoning and save us the superfluous," Lered replied as he adjusted the thin brown leather sash across his chest and the woven rope belt fitted with scabbard and sword to which it was attached.

"Why can you not keep your place in the list? Why must others wait longer while you are granted favor?" Lered finished with something of a challenge. He did not want to appear to be playing favorites with Keeres by ordering this unusual assembly.

Keeres knew that the extraordinary circumstances surrounding this child would raise far more discussion than he wished to provoke. He wished to satisfy the essential question without raising 100 more.

"Um, ah, yes," Keeres mumbled while struggling to keep his composure, aware that only a few key words now stood between him and the child.

"Go on," Lered sped him forward with a measure of impatience.

Keeres took a deep breath and assumed a wide stance for maximum affect, "As the council knows, I have been a watcher for seven years in addition to my work in the stables, and brought many a child from the wall into our great city. During that time I have unfortunately witnessed a few losses; wandering beasts have scented our young and made an end to them. On this day I feared the same, turning the fourth wall to the sound of a distant snarling. With sinking heart I raced along the wall sword in hand, not knowing if I would be too late or if I could intercept the beasts. Gray wolves they were and none too few, being numbered at half a dozen."

Keeres was not normally a man of great flamboyance, but he was outdoing himself with this impassioned plea. In his desire to impress, his overstated attempt at a formality with which he was not skilled was becoming comic. He vented his boiling emotions by waving and motioning in an exaggerated manner attempting to emphasize the import of the event.

"Kkkhh," one of the council members choked back a snicker. They all sensed that they were witnessing a bit of theater from this likable but desperate soul and more than a few smirks were now visible among them. Keeres finished in a flurry of bluster having trouble deciding where to take a breath, desperate for a favorable outcome.

"I was glad to reach the child in time enough and the beasts were dispatched. I snatched up the child and wept from relief while the child slept in trust. So, presently being near the top of the list and given these unusual circumstances, I petition this wise council to grant my request for adoption of the child."

"Dispatched? Just like that! Extraordinary!" Lered grinned. He was a bit incredulous. "I had no idea you were such a fine swordsman! Did you suffer injury?"

"None, fine Council Chair."

Keeres remained in heroic character, puffy chested with arms thrown back.

"And the child?"

"Not a mark on her."

"Extraordinary indeed! One man with a sword against six agile beasts. Keeres you are a fine citizen, but has your eagerness to enter fatherhood embellished your story a bit?" Lered's skepticism was showing.

Keeres before the council

"Your own officers have already verified the kill. The blood is fresh."

Keeres countered the skepticism by pulling his blood stained sword from its scabbard, and a nod from the ranking lieutenant who had just returned from the kill site, per Keeres instructions, confirmed the statement. This corroborating evidence ended the lighthearted amusement of the moment as the council recognized the account, however bizarre, was indeed truthful. The eyebrows of all were now raised, save one.

"All very compelling and my empathy is with Keeres, but we have laws and procedures for a purpose. Each of us knows the consequences of granting exceptions. We will soon be doing nothing except hearing early morning petitions, each citizen begging for the council's indulgence in this or that extraordinary matter!" Darrsce, the newest member of the council protested.

Darrsce had received his appointment to the council in large part due to his careful positioning, promises and payoffs. The council position was his latest attempt to win the respect of a father who cared nothing for him, or anything for that matter besides his own precious wealth.

"Your point is well taken Darrsce and it will be duly considered in our deliberation. However, in fairness it would be best for you to recuse yourself from this decision, seeing that you are on the adoption list ahead of Keeres. You have a clear conflict of interest," the Chair commented as he glanced down at the list in front of him.

Darrsce held his composure but burned beneath his polite grin. He had also gained a high spot on the adoption list through various maneuvers and blackmailing and was none too pleased to suffer a setback. The lack of children in his home was just another aching wound in his paternal relationship, his father often chiding him for having no legal heir. To his father it was not about a loving relationship with a child, it was about the secure passage of wealth within the family.

"I recuse myself," Darrsce conceded with a forced smile.

He knew his reputation as an impartial player in the council power structure would be damaged if he did not.

"But mark my words; this council shall see no end of frivolous matters if this petition is approved."

The council of nine, now eight looked back and forth among themselves with a few twisted lips, a few shrugged shoulders and a mumble or two between them.

Lered spoke, "I am the father of five, grandfather of 12, great grandfather of two and never in my years have I experienced such a significant play of destiny among *my* offspring. I am not a lover of signs or omens but I have lived long enough not to discount them out of hand. I move to approve the petition. Those on the list whom Keeres has overtaken in this instance can be compensated by a waiving of the waiting period typical for subsequent children. Besides, a man should have some reward for accomplishing a feat that would be difficult for five. Give the child to Keeres."

The arrangement suited all members except Darrsce and left none with awkward political consequences. So, in deference to the faithful watcher Keeres, the petition was approved.

"Well done," congratulated the clerk as he handed the sleeping child to the exiting Keeres, "a bit overplayed for my taste, but cleverly maneuvered none the less."

Keeres nodded politely, wishing to depart before further questions came upon him.

"I'll make these half-truths right in due time," he said to the child as he mounted his horse with a twinge of conscience.

He would begin by sharing the entire ordeal with Locenes very shortly.

The indignant nursemaid, just having learned of the outcome, stood slump shouldered and wide mouthed at the Capitol steps as Keeres exited.

"Yey ho!" Keeres gave a wink and a shout to her as he rode away, child in arms.

2

"Papa! Help Papa!!!" Selah shouted in desperation as she dangled upside down from the horse, one foot caught in the stirrup and her loosely curled dark hair brushing against the stone street in front of their house.

"Selah!" Locenes looked through the front window to see the dangling child. "Keeres! Selah needs help!"

"Aha!" Keeres burst through the front door to find the topsy-turvy child, almost knocking down a passerby, so close were those houses built to the street.

"Papa, get me down!" Selah pleaded as Windspeed, their dark brown horse, stood idly by.

"Hmmm. And how is it that you find yourself in such a predicament as this?" Keeres asked as he stood stroking his chin as though deciphering a puzzle. He knew the answer but wanted to hear it from her and calmly waited as Selah sniffed at his inverted boot laces.

"Papa! My leg is all twisty!" the little munchkin pleaded. Her bright green eyes began to well up with tears.

"Keeres, get her loose at once!" Locenes scolded them both from the front window.

Just then, their intended traveling companion Noble arrived, "Well, what have we here?"

"I'm afraid our novice rider was a bit too eager to start the journey and attempted to mount Windspeed by herself, in spite of my explicit instructions," Keeres explained as he righted the woozy Selah, setting her upon Windspeed's back and giving her twisted ankle a good rubbing.

Her blood began to drain back to its familiar course and her fair pudgy cheeks regained their normal tone.

"I am eager as well, Selah! We shall be on the trail in no time at all!" Noble consoled. "However, we'll see how eager you are to ride after six weeks in the saddle bouncing along the Tolis trails."

"If I had to guess, I'd bet she'll weather it better than I," Keeres interjected, hands on Selah's knees.

"Are you sure we won't get lost?" Selah fretted as Keeres lowered her to the street.

"How can a man get lost in a place such as Maraldia?" Noble chuckled. "I have been trying to get lost for 30 years and have not succeeded so far!"

His deep set blue eyes sparkled in the morning sun, closely cropped beard circling his sun weathered face. Noble did, in fact, make a living out of trying to get lost, as it were. A rugged man of just 33 years, Noble had braved ocean tempest, mountain cold and most expeditions in between.

"Don't worry Selah, our entire journey will be bounded by the great flat vertical slab that is the Tolis Mountain on our north and the edge of the Great Ocean 34 stanion to the south. It is very wet, you can't miss it."

Selah giggled as Noble melted her apprehension, "If it were any simpler it would hardly be worth the trip."

"Are the supplies at your shop?" Keeres was almost ready to go.

"Yes, I've prepared a satchel of supplies for each horse. We'll stop there on our way out of the city," Noble informed.

Unlike other explorers in Maraldia who were enabled to pursue their wanderlust due to a generous inheritance, Noble carved out a meager living making and selling wilderness supplies. Maps and compasses and lightweight gear of every sort decorated his modest shop. However, if it were only for the wide selection of goods, Noble's shop would be judged the poorest. In spite of this limitation Noble's business thrived, not due to his exceptional stock, but due to his exceptional storytelling born of his own experiences and seasoned with not a little imagination. Customers would bypass more handsome shops to patronize Noble's because his word paintings reminded them why they wanted to purchase such obscure items in the first place. Nine months of business gave Noble enough means to explore for three months and three months of exploring gave him enough stories to last the next nine.

"I'll accompany you to Noble's shop," Locenes informed Keeres as she mounted Arrow, the second family horse. She wished to prolong her moments with her only child. "Selah will ride with me."

When they arrived at Noble's shop Keeres struggled to lift the heavy satchel upon his horse.

"Let me help you with that Keeres."

Noble's help made the task effortless for Keeres and he remembered that Noble's strength was not of the type you see in athletes with finely sculpted muscles. His was born of wilderness hardship, excessive hours of physical labor and leanness of food and rest. Any self-assured athlete taking Noble for an easy mark would soon find himself in deeper waters than he had wished.

"Well done, Noble. If we encounter a bear I shall refer him directly to you," Keeres joked, a bit embarrassed at his comparative weakness.

Loading up at Noble's shop

Noble grinned and gave Keeres a nod, "I think we are ready, everyone say your goodbyes," Noble directed as he tightened the last satchel strap on his horse, Northsong, "and if we are so fortunate as to encounter a bear we shall eat well for many days, and Selah shall have a new coat!" Noble spoke from experience.

"Did you ever eat a bear?" Selah was filled with wonder.

During the long nine-month winters of Maraldia, Selah would always look for ways to provoke Noble into a delicious tale upon visiting his shop.

"Well, certainly! We were *both* hungry, but I was hungrier." Noble made it seem like an everyday event as he gave her a wink.

"What happened?" Selah's eyes were getting wide and she felt this was going to be a wonderful trip.

"The bear story will be more interesting if I save it for when we are in the forest."

Selah instinctively scrunched her shoulders together as a shiver ran down her spine at the thought of seeing a real bear in a real forest.

"Ok," she managed, now a little uncertain about hearing the bear story.

"Keeres, she is only a 7-year-old girl. Keep that in mind as you select your foolish man-play each day," Locenes voiced her apprehensions while helping Selah mount Windspeed, Keeres already seated and ready to receive her.

Keeres did not answer, but bent down to plant an exaggeratedly passionate kiss on her worried lips.

"Ewww," Selah objected and looked away. Locenes feigned a protest, but not so much as to disengage.

"All will be well. We will see you in six weeks, just in time for the festival." Keeres straightened with a smile as Locenes regained her composure, folded her arms, and glancing around the street to see who had been watching. She nodded her head in agreement.

Without further delay the trio set out, winding their way through the neighborhoods and parks at a comfortable trot as Locenes headed back home in the other direction.

"Selah, look at the rafts! There are races on the Elif today, see over there!" Keeres pointed them out to Selah as they crossed the river Elif which entered the west city wall near the gate where they would be exiting in a few minutes. That semielliptical wall surrounded the city, nine paces tall all around and beginning and ending against the sheer face of the great Tolis mountains.

"They race from this bridge, around the southward river bend mid-city, out the south wall and all the way to the ocean 20 stanion away. I did it once myself as young boy," Noble added his colorful commentary.

"Did you win?" Selah was sure he must have.

"Well, not exactly," Noble said as he lowered his head a bit and glanced over at Selah with a wry smile.

"Tell it! Tell it!" Selah squealed and bounced up and down in the saddle anticipating a thrilling tale.

"Well, OK. But it is a very boring story," Noble teased and rolled his eyes.

"Tell it please!" Selah wriggled.

Noble began, "Well, it was when I was 12 years old and had worked all summer on my raft, fitting the sail and rudder and rigging. I was hoping to win the prize money so I could buy some expensive climbing gear that I'd been eyeing for a long time. Everything was ready and all the boys age 12-14 were lined up in the river on their rafts at this very bridge waiting for the starting whistle. A rope was stretched bank to bank and each pilot clung to it from the back of their rafts, keeping themselves in place. When the race began I seemed to be going nowhere fast while all the other rafts sped away. After struggling to get any speed for the first few minutes of the race, I discovered that some older boys who had been jeering me earlier had tied three sea anchors to the bottom of my raft. By the time I dove in with my knife to cut them loose the closest raft was nearly out of sight. I spent the rest of the race catching up, passing one raft after another. I even took the time to toss one of those older boys off his raft along the way. HA!" Noble gave a little shout of exhilaration at the memory of it.

"Well, with only half a stanion to go I was beginning to overtake the last raft, and the crowd that had gathered at the shore was cheering me on. They had seen my story unfold and rooted for the underdog, some riding horseback along the riverbank the entire way. As I started to pass the last raft I caught the eye of the pilot, a slender boy my age. I did not know him well, but remembered seeing him at the funeral procession of his father earlier that year and knew that he had dropped out of school to provide for his mother and three younger siblings. I had been hoping to take the race prize money to buy climbing gear, he was fighting for bread. I saw the panicked look in his eye as I approached and heard his mother cheering him on from the east bank. I maneuvered up next to him like I was going to interfere with his rigging, but 'accidentally,'" Noble made little quote signs in the air, "fell off the back of my raft. My raft finished second without me."

Selah studied the rafts beneath them now with more imagination, wondering what stories might be unfolding that day.

"Well done, Noble. The lack of that day's prize money has not seemed to hinder your exploring ambitions," Keeres commented.

"No. I've done alright," Noble remarked and smiled as they cleared the bridge on their way to the western gate, now following the cobblestone street that paralleled the southern bank of the Elif.

They road in silence for the better part of half an hour occupied with thoughts of Noble's rafting story and observing all the activity along the river.

"How far will we go today? I'm hungry." Selah's mind turned to the magnitude of the journey ahead as they exited the west gate to a thin forest, ever thickening as they followed the Tolis trail.

"Only three stanion to the waterfall. We'll stop there for lunch. We'll do another 25 stanion before we set up camp. Four, maybe five hours of riding a day ought to get us where we want to go with plenty of time for exploring along the way. Plenty of time to make Selah a bearskin coat," Noble teased.

Selah immediately sharpened her focus, such as it was in Maraldia, for sneaky bears ready to pounce upon them. The forest had thickened now and provided ample cover for forest animals.

"Oh!! I love the waterfall!" Selah forced her mind away from bears and onto the distant sound of crashing water.

She had never been there but had heard marvelous descriptions from Keeres. Twenty minutes later they were at the lake into which the waterfall plunged.

"Let's stop up ahead on the western edge of the lake at the base of the Tolis," Noble instructed.

"It's so loud! And I can smell the water in the air!" Selah gushed.

The waterfall was a gigantic crashing blur to them, far across the lake and plunging out from a mighty crack in the sheer face of the Tolis 100 paces above. It was the life spring for the lake, the Elif which it fed, and the entire city of Maraldia.

"Can we go fishing?" Selah had never been.

"I have the gear, can you find a worm? What's more, can you skewer the guts of the friendly worm with a pointy hook?" Noble tested Selah's mettle.

The lake at the base of the waterfall was expansive and offered plenty of grassy shallows where fish could be found.

"I killed lots of worms at the stables." Selah was proud to show off her skills and remind Noble that she worked around dirty places that many girls would disdain.

"Very well," Noble acknowledged with a serious tone. Keeres grinned.

Within a few minutes they had reached the spot well known to Noble.

"Time for a little fishing and a little lunch," Keeres directed as he swung himself down from Windspeed and hoisted Selah as well.

"Papa is this the Tolis?" Selah patted the sheer rock face with her hand and looked straight up.

She had never even been to the base of the mountain within the city walls. A stanion worth of forest cushioned the metropolis within the wall from the stark face of that mountain and Keeres had never adventured there with her.

"It's a little piece of it." Keeres was enjoying her discoveries.

"How high is it?" Selah craned her neck upward.

"Four stanion straight up from where you stand. But that's the highest spot. As we ride along the next few weeks to the west the mountain descends all the way down to the forest level. But it rises straight out of the ground like this the whole way, like a straight solid wall. It protects us from the winter winds." Keeres was feeling very fatherly and wise.

"Momma said you made her stay into the winds. She said you were a little crazy," Selah smirked.

"When we were young we traveled to the western woods, hiking and enjoying its beauty. I purposely kept us longer than planned, into the beginning of the winds just to see it, to feel it. Your mother was fascinated at the transformation of the forest," Keeres explained.

Keeres did not mention that many had died trying that stunt, but Locenes had no fear with Keeres leading. She loved his adventurous spirit and that he was always asking questions about life and meaning and existence. That is why he became a watcher so long ago; it was his fascination with the mystical.

"Tell me about the winds," Selah continued her quest for stories.

"Noble tells it best," Keeres deferred as he made preparations for lunch, winking at Noble to deliver the description he had heard him give many times to patrons of his shop. The mountain provided a good back rest for Selah as she readied herself for another vicarious adventure.

"Selah, our people live in a tightly circumscribed world as you know, but not without a fight. Our ancestors have attempted without success to establish settlements beyond the shelter of the Tolis. We have farmed and populated lands everywhere the Tolis extends its protective cover, but something has always pressed explorers back home or killed them. What is this 'something', Selah?" Noble engaged his audience.

"The winter winds!" she replied and sat up a little straighter.

The fair city of Maraldia

"Yes indeed," he continued, using his hands and facial expressions to paint a picture. "As autumn grays into winter the faint mixed smell of northern tundra and southern ocean can be perceived in the forest. As the last leaf turns from orange to brown the wind arrives to carry it away. And carry away it does, as breeze grows to gale and from gale to roaring howl. Dry and cold screams the wind from what seems like all directions at once, as the distant northern tundra and warm southern ocean battle with swords of furious air over the forest battlefield." Noble was waxing poetic and Selah listened with rapt attention.

"For a span of three months the serene wood becomes a tumult of soil, leaf, and stick. A truce of stillness and naked cold follows and ice beyond that. Unhurried pellets of crystalline ice, fine as salt, fall slowly and steadily for perhaps 12 days,

~ 30 ~

burying all to twice the depth of a horse's bridle. Four months still as a photograph typically follow until warmer southern breezes begin the melting, ushering in five to six weeks of warm rains and floods. Only a long winter sleep spares any forest dwelling creatures in those environs and we Maraldians are not endowed with such gifts. We, therefore, furiously explore everywhere and settle nowhere, save under the protective cover of the Tolis," he finished the description he had polished well over the years.

"Are you going to try to and make it through the winds?" Selah had heard Noble speak of it before.

"It's a tantalizing challenge. I know that once a man is out from the cover of the Tolis, a northward journey means negotiating the thick forest of sparse trails which eventually thins to vast barren tundra. Several have gone as far as one could in the three months between winters and others have died in the winds trying to go farther."

Noble ripped away a bite of some chewy dried salt beef, "Yes, a northern expedition intrigues me most and the more the practical considerations mount against such a venture the more it intrigues me." The subject was close to Nobles heart.

"Are you gonna do it?" He had not answered Selah's question and she knew it.

"Someday I will go further north than any Maraldian. Someday," he replied, weighing his resolve carefully.

"Can I come, please?" Selah's imagination was on fire.

"Let's enjoy today's adventure first," said Noble, dodging a promise. However, he gave her a wink to indicate he would welcome the company of such a kindred spirit.

Those next six weeks of riding, climbing, swimming, hunting, and storytelling surpassed anything that Keeres had been planning since the day he brought Selah home, and he had planned much. Years of schooling could not do as much for Selah as those six weeks, and they all returned home exhausted but delighted.

"Momma!" Selah dropped herself down from Windspeed like a pro and ran for her mother.

"Oh baby!" Locenes cried and wrapped her arms around the smelly child, relieved to see her safe and healthy, though a wee bit thinner. "Let's get you clean and fed. You have made it back just in time for the festival!"

That evening was spent listening to Selah recount her adventures to friends and neighbors as Locenes filled the house with the smell of fresh bread and pot roast. As the moon rose the house quieted and Selah happily darted to her familiar comfortable bed.

"Neighhhhhh! Prrrrt! Pbbb! Whineee!" Selah played and pranced with her wooden horses. She had learned to amuse herself in those pleasant hours after friends were shooed away to their own apartments while mother and father sat talking by the fire.

As she played in her room on the weathered wood floor by candle light she noticed a flicker of shadow on the wall. Selah knew the tricks of dancing candlelight and was not easily fooled into a false start, but this shadow brought her immediately to her feet,

"Papa?"

She looked around the room expecting Papa to be playing some game but he was within sight through the small corridor sitting by the fire with mama. Having looked under the bed and into the dresser to find nothing she grabbed her wooden horses and quickly jumped into bed, pulling the blankets up to her chin. With quiet neighing and prancing she continued with the wooden horses, but only for a moment. Again the unusual flicker.

"Papa?!" a little more panicked but still a whisper. "Who is it?!"

She drew the blankets up to just under her eyes and covered her forehead with the pillow until she was no more than a sliver of a child.

"Papa, you are scaring me!" she whispered in case Papa was sneaking up on her.

Her heart pounded as her eyes raced around the room. She did not want to prove herself a coward by running to her parents at every notion of a phantom but her courage was at its limit. From the corner of the dimly lit room, just beyond the haze of her Maraldian nearsightedness emerged an adult form. She tried to scream but like a mute dream, no voice would come. The figure floated across the room, reached for her head, and opened his mouth to speak.

3

Selah awoke wondering if it had been nothing more than a fantastic dream. She remembered the terror of the tall form gliding across the room and the unexpected calm that spilled over her as the man uncloaked his head to reveal the most peaceful face she had ever seen. She had been so transfixed by that face that fear was immediately replaced with longing and she reached out her curious hand to touch the broad bright smile of this stranger. One touch revealed that this was no phantom but real flesh and bone, perhaps the most real she had ever seen. The face even appeared, for lack of a better term, "bright". Not quite glowing and not pale or white (his skin was darker than her own) but somehow vivid and clear beyond the ability of the dim candle across the room to illuminate. He knelt at her bedside for a moment and she perceived that he must be very tall since he needed to sit back on his heels and nearly double over at the waist to rest his forearms on her bed.

Though the face brought peace, the words did not.

"Peace, child. You are chosen and loved by the family of which we are. My name is Rivoas and I bring a message for the people and a mission for you."

Immediately something leaped in her chest and she wished to question from where he had been sent and who was "the family" but could not bring herself to interrupt.

"Selah, all is well and all will be well but there are times of testing ahead. This island city will not survive until the next moon. You must bring this message to the people. You will be a dividing sword to this place, for all will not welcome your message. Every spirit will know the voice of truth you bring, but many have louder voices within."

Even such a startling message did not disturb the peace Selah was absorbed in.

"All is well and all will be well," she repeated.

"Yes," he continued, a fatherly smile on his face, "you will see me and must follow bringing as many as will come. Before the evening on the last day of the festival we must depart. The next day's sunrise will find no living thing in Maraldia."

"But all will be well, right?" her confidence shaken slightly by the idea of no living thing in the bustling city.

"Yes, as all is well."

"And Momma and Papa? All will be well with them?" her thoughts running ahead.

"Peace, child."

"And Skud, that nasty boy will never come! He will laugh and pull my hair and make a fuss!" her mind was reeling.

"Peace, peace. As a sign of trust I will soon give you a gift and you will know what to do."

With these words he covered his head in the dark cloak and reached out his hand to cover her eyes. His touch made her draw a deep breath and she was filled with a sense of wonder like a child that has never seen an ocean and for the first time rises over a hill to a vast panorama of sand and shore, tall grass, salt breeze and crashing waves. As she exhaled deep and long, this wonder lay her down into thick sleep and he was gone.

Now as the morning sun glinted through her window she wondered if it had indeed been nothing more than a dream brought on by Noble's fabulous tales and that second piece of cherry pie snuck away just before bedtime. She lay for a while rolling this "dream" over in her head and watching a songbird peck at a berry on the bush through the misaligned window shade.

"Hello, birdie! Aren't you a pretty birdie!" she whispered to the creature.

As she mused, it occurred to her that the songbird was unusually stunning in color and form. Every jerky motion of the eye and head was perceivable; the gradient of color in the wing and beak was remarkable. She felt as if she could reach out and touch it without leaving her bed.

"This is a wonderful dream!" Selah whispered to her wooden horses as she began to notice that her whole house looked different. "I can see all the way into the kitchen and last night's dishes left out to dry. I can even count the number of forks in the basket!" she informed the horses.

Indeed, everything seemed visible in high definition.

"Let's go explore the dream world." Selah put the horses in her pajama pocket and peeled off her bed sheets, tiptoeing into the kitchen so as not to bring a sleepy mother and father into her dream.

All things near and far were somehow in perfect focus. She began to breathe a little faster and had the urge to run but instead composed herself, put on her slippers and edged out the front door.

"Wwwwwow!" The sight that met Selah upon opening the door nearly knocked her off her feet and left her mouth and eyes gaping wide.

Instead of the usual fuzzy brightness of a clear day in Maraldia with only a handful of neighboring houses or shops visible, Selah could see every building from her own to the town square a full stanion away in magnificent detail.

"Wwwwwhoa!" The cobblestone streets were exceptionally beautiful as she studied for a moment every detail of their puzzled fittings and marveled at the sunlight sparkling off each dewy facet; a sprawling river of stone glistening in the sun, met on each side by fieldstone houses each of two stories.

She saw her friend Sardis at the bakery two blocks away.

"Sardis!" she shouted waving her arms frantically.

There was no response except from the old neighbor lady, "What in the world is all the shouting about? Do your parents know you're in the street wearing your pajamas?"

The round old woman squinted out the front window of her house, head framed by merry shutters and a colorful flowerbox. Selah made no reply. She saw one of Skud's raggedy gang sneaking into the alley intent on stealing some raspberries.

"You better get out of Mrs. Turneur's raspberries or I'll tell!" she called, but he just looked around in bewilderment at the sound of the invisible voice too distant for his poor vision.

However, the greatest surprise greeted Selah as she turned toward the north, a sight filling her with both fright and awe.

"Aahhh!" Selah gasped.

The gigantic expanse of the Tolis mountains seemed ready to swallow the city in a single gulp. At this spectacle she stopped breathing and began to tremble, staring nearly straight up into the black flat wall whose uniformity was only interrupted by thousands of wavy undulations as the rock slanted imperceptibly away from the city to the north and up to the blue sky toward the peak.

"Momma?!" Selah whispered, wondering when she would wake, not certain any more if she were in a dream.

Selah's mind was reeling as she stumbled back a few steps, eyes fixed on the Tolis. She halted her retreat upon spying something peculiar moving in the rock. As she stopped to really focus on this distant sight, which was more than a stanion away and 100 paces high up into the rock face, she recognized the form of the man at her bedside smiling down upon her.

"It's the man…the man in my room!"

She pinched herself without taking her eyes off Rivoas. It was not a dream, and she had received the gift of which he had spoken; sight twice as keen as the best bird of prey. She could see him standing in the opening of a small cave and remembered his instructions to bring as many as would come.

"Just, umm, ah, look…," was all that she could now manage pointing frantically and beginning to cry.

Just then her sweet mother came from the house to find the frantic Selah stammering and shaking. Keeres joined momentarily and tried calming her enough to make sense of the babblings.

"He said to escape…," she blubbered.

"Who said?" her father probed?

"Him!" she said, pointing.

"Where? North? There is no one! Where?" Keeres did not understand her vacant pointing. "Does this have something to do with Noble's stories?"

Her mother perceived that they were beginning to draw a crowd and the family retreated hastily indoors.

In that small curious crowd happened to be a man of some standing, a renowned explorer and contemporary, if not rival, of Noble. This man of means did not like the fact that his countrymen preferred the tales of a lowly shopkeeper to his professional and scientific work. Stylish and handsome, clean shaven and tall, he observed Selah's spectacle as one observes the antics of zoo monkeys excited by a delivery of bananas. Superior, aloof, arms folded and a comfortable distance away he welcomed the brief diversion from his busy morning. However, his condescending amusement with the strange little girl turned to riveted interest as he picked out the words "north" and "escape" from Selah's bizarre monologue. He had seen these words among some ancient faded cave writings he discovered on a recent northern expedition. He had not published his findings yet, preferring to make more extended searches in that same area in hopes of producing Maraldia's most significant historical find ever without the pesky competition of amateurs. He hoped that this achievement would finally win for him the prestige he had sought for so long. Prestige and respect from his peers but mostly from the father who belittled his every advance; the father who laughed at his scientific explorations as poor business and spit on the ground when learning of his appointment to the Maraldian council. Darrsce made a note of the direction in which the little girl had been pointing, the address of her house, and the mention of Noble. He would without a doubt be making a visit to this family very soon.

4

Across the street at the local schoolhouse, Skud jostled his cohort Jojus, "Hey, look out the wind'er there! That little Selah freak is runnin' around the street in her 'jamas!"

Skud was in summer school with a handful of others to revisit lessons ignored the previous year. Jojus attended with Skud not because he had to, but because he enjoyed it and this trait had earned him the reputation as gang intellectual.

"She's bustin' out cryin'. Here comes her Ma!" Jojus joined the commentary.

Mr. Bagawind had not yet begun his lecture and so excused the classroom murmurings.

"Ha!" Skud vented his amusement, then losing interest turned to Jojus, "it's a good thing this be the last day a school. I already missed a week's worth a good thievin' from all the sellers settin' up their street booths." Artisans and vendors of all types had begun days ago to arrange their colorful booths and displays for the upcoming weeklong festival.

"I know. My little sister spent her whole day yesterday running up and down the street to all her friends' houses tasting candies and desserts baked for the festival while you and me sat in this dungeon." Jojus tried to join the mood.

"You ain't gotta be here. Go git yerself some candies if you want it!" Skud sulked, knowing that he was missing all the pre-festival excitement. Societies and fraternities of every sort had been for weeks making preparations for the final day's parade. Musicians practiced songs which inspired spirited street dancing from young and old.

"We're not missing anything, Skud. All the contests and excitement starts tonight," Jojus replied, deciding to adopt a conciliatory tone.

The festival was indeed a sight to behold, the highlight of the Maraldian calendar. All manner of frivolous and tawdry goods were for sale, pleasing to the eye and in an impulsive moment purchased by the happy-go-lucky citizen. Incessant contests to determine the best singer, dancer, eater, runner, juggler, wrestler and so on drew crowds to the city square at all hours creating an ongoing clamor which made the side street bystander eager to find out what he was missing. Serious commerce also was traditionally conducted by the businessmen during this week. Contracts and alliances for the coming year were established or renewed over wine and beer in the festive atmosphere.

"Ahem, let us begin." Mr. Bagawind brought the class to attention.

Skud took this redirection as an opportunity to whack Jojus in the back of the head like boys will do, knowing there would be no window for retaliation. Mr. Bagawind scolded with nothing more than a raised eyebrow.

"Since the festival begins tonight, today's lecture will be a history of its origin," Bagawind began.

Skud let his forehead hit the desk surface with a loud thud and proceeded to make snoring noises, to the great amusement of his chuckling classmates.

"Do you have a problem, Skud? Would you like to come back next week and spend the festival here with me in the classroom? The same offer goes for all of your snickering audience," Mr. Bagawind threatened as he looked around the room. Everyone sat up straight, including a reluctant Skud.

"Now, each of you knows the modern customs of the festival, the games and pageants and music, but who can tell me something of its origin?"

Mr. Bagawind attempted to engage his lethargic class on this final day.

"I can!" bubbled Velcer, a small boy who was bright but sickly. He had missed his lessons during the school year due to illness, not apathy.

"Please do," smiled Bagawind.

"Our loud and tumultuous modern celebration began, according to the histories, as a simple ceremony to honor the Givers," Velcer proudly exercised his adult sized vocabulary.

"Yes, yes, well said, Velcer. Now this reference to the Givers is born from the old superstition that a superior race of some kind sustains Maraldia via the gifting of children outside the city wall each morning, correct?" Bagawind gathered steam.

"Well, yes, I guess so," Velcer hedged.

"You do not seem so certain, Velcer," Bagawind questioned as he turned away to the window.

"Well…" Velcer swallowed hard, "Some people don't think it's a superstition. Some of our poets say we are a city of orphans, looking for our parents. That's why we are always exploring everywhere."

"Do you believe such things?" questioned Bagawind, hands clasped behind his back looking away from the class. "Do you believe in unseen super beings?"

"I don't know," Velcer spoke slowly and hung his head.

The class was silent, each trying to decide how they would answer and hoping not to be asked.

Mr. Bagawind sensed his chance to educate and began with some common ground, "To be certain, the modern festival does reference the ancient notion of the Givers by way of traditional plays dragged out and retold each year. You have seen them, you have acted in them. The story of a great clash of titans engaged in a struggle for control of the universe with betrayal and sacrifice and all the elements of high drama one would expect in a classic old tale. In the end the wicked are vanquished and the victor begins the world anew." His voice betrayed contempt for these notions.

The class was listening, though Velcer did not look up.

Bagawind continued with condescending tone, "How many of you have already decorated your houses with symbols of this old fable? Grotesque rebels being trodden by the victorious and brightly colored ancients. Sorcerers casting spells and angelic forms holding newborns in outstretched arms. Apple sized shiny globes painted with detailed figures, the entire story in miniature around the circumference. Ever since you were babies the sight of these trinkets filled you with wonder and the anticipation of the coming festival and the retelling of the old story which no educated person believes anymore. Enjoy these stories as quaint reminders of a shared and simple minded history, nothing more."

Bagawind paced quietly to the other side of the room before beginning again, ready to fill the vacuum he had carefully created, "Who can enlighten us with the scientific explanation of Maraldian repopulation?"

All knew, but no one raised a hand.

"Jojus?" Mr. Bagawind tried the back of the class.

"Umm, something about the balance of energy," Jojus offered, looking around self-consciously.

"Yes, very good. That is a beginning," Bagawind filled in the rest, "the process is called life energy balance. We now know that a fixed amount of life energy exists in the universe and that as the dead give up their life energy, new life must emerge. Our scientists have studied centuries of birth and death ratios among men and beasts and conducted thousands of experiments. There is no longer any reasonable doubt as to the validity of these findings."

Velcer raised his hand but did not wait to speak, "Haven't the most recent scientific discoveries brought this theory into question? I read that somewhere."

"There are opponents of progress who will write anything to confuse the issue and hang onto the old fables." Bagawind used his stature as teacher to quell the question without further evaluation of the facts.

Velcer quickly retreated, "Yes, sir."

Across the street, Keeres was also musing about the old tales as Locenes unpacked their festival ornaments. Since the adoption of Selah, Keeres looked on these ornaments with a new curiosity. Though he had accepted the modern theories from his youth, he had a difficult time imagining that nature's life energy balance could disembowel half a dozen gray wolves.

"Has she quieted yet?" Keeres questioned in hushed tones as Locenes stepped out of Selah's room.

"Yes, and she is asking for you. Go speak with her while I make breakfast."

Their eyes met and an understanding passed between them, a mutual acknowledgement that said to them both "so it begins", though neither had the slightest idea what "it" might be. They felt that an anticipated threshold, long awaited, had now been stepped over.

Keeres peeked his head through her door and knocked softly, "Selah?"

"Papa, come papa!" she replied and held arms open wide.

Keeres sat on the bed and embraced her, then wedged his back against the corner of the room into which the bed was pressed. They faced each other cross-legged, holding hands.

"Papa, I'm scared," she began.

"Scared of what, darling? Please tell me everything." He squeezed her fingers.

"The mountain and the man's words! We have to tell everyone and I am too small! Papa will the mountain fall on us?" Her mind was having trouble putting everything in order.

"I am here Selah. Don't be afraid. Let's take one thing at a time. Why are you afraid of the mountain?" His structured approach calmed her.

"I can see it, Papa! I can see everything! The man said he would give me a gift and now I can see everything! But oh, the mountain is so big and I think it is ready to fall on us! He said we have to go north!" Again her mind was a tangle of thoughts.

Keeres wanted mostly to know about the man but he forced himself to keep a single line of questioning. "Selah, you can see the mountain? The mountain is more than a stanion away! Did that boy Skud tell you that the mountain would fall on us?"

"No Papa, I can see it! I can see everything! I saw Sardis down at the baker's shop when I went outside. I could see all the way to the city square! I can see the plates that Momma has in the kitchen right now."

Her last statement about the plates gave Keeres an idea. "Locenes!" he called. "Please choose a certain number of coins from my jar in the kitchen and line them up on the edge of the kitchen table but don't tell us how many."

When she had finished, Keeres continued, "Selah if you can see them, tell me how many coins are on the kitchen table."

Selah relaxed and giggled a little enjoying the game. "Oh Papa, I'm not a baby anymore. There are five coins, two phares, two trindle, and one chamlet, a really old one."

No one Keeres knew could see such small objects from that distance. He asked Locenes if Selah's "guess" was correct. She did not answer but brought the coins to Keeres. "See for yourself."

It was just as Selah had said, down to the old chamlet.

Selah grinned, "Can we do it again? There are 1,2,3,4,5,6,7 eggs on the kitchen counter, there is a fly on the windowsill and a little cherry pie spilled on the floor."

She was proud to show off her new skills. Locenes reported back that all of it was accurate except that the fly was on the move for which Selah gave a running commentary.

"Selah, who is the man you spoke of? What did he say?" Keeres, accepting the miraculous, now moved on with his inquiry.

"Oh, Papa, what about the mountain?" she asked, refusing to let that go.

"Darling, the mountain has been there as long as this city, only you have now seen it as no one ever has. I see no special reason why it should fall upon us today. Tell me about the man," he answered, redirecting her thoughts.

"OK, I guess he didn't actually say it would fall on us. But he said we had to run away and follow him." She was beginning to track with Keeres now.

"Where did he come from? Where did you see him?"

Selah told all about the bright stranger in the room the night before, about how she was afraid to be a little baby and call out for help. She described her peace in spite of his message, the promise of a gift and about the sudden sleep his touch brought upon her.

"And I saw him in the mountain, Papa," she finished.

Just then Locenes entered with hard boiled eggs, cheese and bread. She had been listening to everything. They all sat on the bed but no one ate much.

Their silent contemplation was interrupted by an abrupt knock on the door. Keeres jumped up to answer expecting almost anything, from a bright faced man to a neighbor telling him the mountain was falling down. All seemed equally probable. He was relieved to find that it was just his good friend, Rohon, whom he knew from their years together as fishermen. Rohon stayed to the seas all these years while Keeres moved on to breeding and keeping horses for those who could afford them.

"How goes it, old Rohon, please come in," Keeres quickly adopted a hospitable tone.

"The seas take their toll, Keeres. You were smart to get out young. But it's a living and it's what I know," Rohon spoke as he stepped in and settled into a chair.

Rohon was a short barrel chested man with thick neck, arms, and legs all with plentiful hair contrasting his clean shaven head and chin.   In his youth, Rohon had won the festival wrestling contests 12 years running.   His round face had become wrinkled around the eyes but the brown eyes still twinkled and his friendly smile was a favorite among children. He seemed impatient with the small talk, seeming to have something else on his mind.   He and Keeres had been close confidants on the ships and maintained that relationship all these years sharing political or social hearsay over drinks and making of it what they could.

"Do you have plans for the festival, Rohon?" Keeres queried absentmindedly reaching for some extra eggs and cheese to set before his guest.

Rohon ignored the question, "Keeres, do you think I'm crazy?"

"Yes, since the day I met you." Keeres ate now with greater appetite in the company of his old friend.

"No really, I think the sea is getting to me."

"You just need a break, Rohon. You will feel alright after the festival." Keeres was preoccupied with his own situation too much to pay serious attention to his friend's middle aged insecurities.

"But I see things," Rohon said, a little embarrassed.

Keeres paid more attention given this morning's encounter with people seeing things.

"Explain," he said matter-of-factly, hiding his increased interest.

"Well, ships. Sometimes I see ships."

"You're a fisherman, Rohon. I would think you were crazy if you didn't see ships." Keeres showed a little impatience at his friend's inability to get right to the point, looking to the ceiling and raising a hand in frustration.

"No, no. When I am fishing late into the night or early before sunrise; large ships not like our little schooners. I'd say a full 50 paces in length. But I don't see so well in the dark," he was excited now for a chance to tell a trusted friend and spoke quickly.

"Has anyone else seen them?" Keeres wondered if his friend really was crazy. First of all a boat would have to be very close for any Maraldian to see it and secondly the Maraldians never build a ship beyond 30 paces.

"A couple guys saw things but they were either drunk or half asleep at the time. I've only been seein' 'em in the last two weeks. Just tried to forget about it until this morning when we set sail before sunrise. The fog was pretty thick and we had pushed about two stanion into it. While I was setting the nets I saw something moving against the direction of the fog so I stared real hard, waiting, quiet. Then I saw it, the bow of what must have been a ship 50 paces long, two, three seconds then completely gone."

Keeres was listening intently now, "Did you see the figurehead below the bowsprit; a mermaid or warrior? What was carved there?"

Keeres was hoping to match the ship with some he had seen before. Replicas of old ships certain wealthy clients kept just for pleasure.

"Yes, the entire front of the ship was carved into a figure of some sort," Rohon recalled.

"Draw what you remember on this scrap."

Keeres slid the paper and pencil to his friend.

Rohon carefully began to etch out the figurehead of that ship with pencil and paper, brooding over every line while Keeres played with the festival ornaments on the table. These ornaments captivated him now more than ever as the morning with Selah had unfolded. He studied the sphere with the ancient mythical story around the circumference; a clash of good and evil in miniature. He did not even understand half of what was painted on that little ball handed down to him from many generations.

Rohon finished as best he could and slid the paper over to Keeres, "There you go old friend, can you make heads or tails of that?"

Keeres glanced at the paper then quickly to the ornament. His stare went vacant as he raised his eyes to Rohon. Rohon's penciled ship figurehead was the exact image of the ancient wicked sorcerer on the old festival ornament in his now quivering hand.

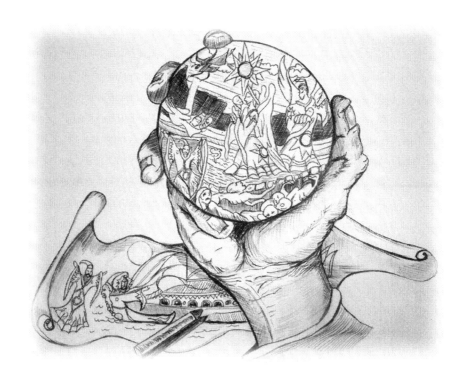

Keeres' discovery

Keeres was not ready to unload his head full of confused fact and mythology into the lap of Rohon and quickly recovered, brandished a smile at his friend saying, "Probably a private ship. Some of my clients have them but you must be mistaken about the size."

Rohon seemed eager for confirmation of his sanity and left it at that.

"Yes, you're probably right."

After they had traded a few additional barbs and backslaps Rohon took his leave, "Hope to see you at the festival, Keeres."

Keeres did want to question his friend further after having time to sort things out, "Perhaps a drink at the Winter Winds?"

"Only one?" questioned Rohon.

"Depends who's paying," quipped Keeres, "I'll keep an eye out for you."

Rohon stepped out with a wink.

Selah spent the rest of the day working with Keeres preparing horses and carriages for city officials who would be using them for their various parties that evening. Both were too preoccupied in thought to speak much for the first few hours until Keeres broke the silence, "Selah, we must not speak to anyone of these things, at least for now. Tomorrow you will lead me to the man."

Selah could barely endure this waiting, this hiding. Whenever a friend passed by at a distance she had an urge to wave and shout and would only catch herself after the initial lunge.

Those nearby thought her a bit jumpy, not seeing the reason for her start. Indeed she was jumpy, eyes darting to and fro taking in all the new information which until today was beyond the haze of her nearsightedness. The mental effort required to keep her composure was exhausting and when her work was complete she quickly fell asleep several hours earlier than usual.

Across the street Skud was nowhere near ready for bedtime. In fact, the 12-year-old could not be said to have ever had a bedtime. Thin and raggedy, thick shocks of tussled hair hanging in his brown eyes and dirty calloused hands completed the picture of this street urchin. His mother died when he was a baby and his father, Stohl, had never worked since. Truthfully he had never really worked and stayed afloat on the generosity of others or via conniving and trickery. A scrap here or a chamlet there. Sometimes the sale of a hand-me-down. Sometimes a bit of thievery. Stohl looked the part of a vagabond with unkempt dark beard, receding hairline partially covered by an old fisherman's cap, spindly thin limbs hidden under threadbare clothes. His home was kept in a similar level of disrepair with hardly a clean or unbroken item in the dark rooms.

"Skud, wha'd you bring back from the square today?" Stohl demanded.

Skud was proud of his take, "One o' them lady dolls with a fancy outfit and all. Got it when the vender looked away at the wrestlin' contest, and I got some pork strips, close-up shop giveaways."

"Gimmy that." Stohl swiped at the food, missing. Skud laid it on the table taking one for himself.

"I don't like you takin' handouts boy. It shames me. You steal it clean next time."
Stohl considered stealing as a craft and therefore respectable in some twisted sense.

"You need do better 'an 'at tomorrow. You know this is our biggest take 'o the year this festival week. Quit wastin' yer time with those no good friends a yers and get down to business, or you'll be looking fer a new roof."

Stohl went for the rest of the pork and with one motion let his open hand slap Skud across the face before grabbing it.

"Get yerself down to business son."

Skud barely looked at him. In reality there was not much threat in the loss of a roof. Since the age of eight Skud was primary breadwinner in that home and could provide for himself easily enough, and any friend would afford him a roof. But the city was small and it would be hard to hide very long from a bully father who was still a couple heads taller.

The next day's fog was certainly ideal for Skud's business. The second day of the festival meant that the shopkeepers were a bit less attentive and the fog would make for excellent cover.

"Jojus, get yer ugly pig face over here!" Skud called to his cohort.

Jojus lived with his mother a few doors down and was just poking his head out the front door as Skud approached.

"Why you gotta call me names first thing in the morning? Besides, yer the ugly pig face. What the heck happened to you?"

Skud rubbed his bruised chin, "Whada' ya think?"

"Old man again, eh. What did you do to wind him up this time?" Jojus queried.

"Nothin' as usual. Hurry up and put on yer makeup sister, we need to git to work before this fog lifts."

Jojus grabbed a small backpack on the floor, "Bye, Ma!" he shouted, not waiting for a reply and tripped out the door over a small stray dog, landing flat on his face.

"What the...!?"

Skud fell down himself from the laughter, rolling on his back in the street. Jojus brought himself to a kneeling position and took a swing but Skud was too quick for that, rolling away to continue his merriment.

"Look he's hurt, you pig face."

Skud finally composed himself and attended to the limping dog.

"I didn't do anything!" Jojus denied, "Never touched him."

Skud was not listening but pulled a small piece of yesterday's pork from his pocket.

The mangy beast gobbled it up and licked Skud's fingers, "There ya go boy. Watch out for that pig face Jojus and you be all right."

Skud inspected the gimpy paw and found it lame, probably born that way. He rubbed noses with the mutt and let him go.

"Come on Skud the fog's lifting," implored Jojus as he dusted himself off.

They set off down the street, limping dog in tow. By the time they got to the city square all hope of using the fog to their advantage had literally evaporated. Cursing, they perused the square looking for easy targets. While doing so Skud noticed Selah as she inspected the same style of doll he had stolen yesterday. She had come to the square with Locenes during the fog which made her new vision less of a marvel. She had not yet noticed its clearing, being entranced with the beautiful wares under the booth canopies. Locenes chatted a few booths away.

"You ain't never gittin' one of those missy, your Papa's a commoner." Skud kept a serious look for maximum affect. "You might as well go home now."

Skud always relished opportunities to pull Selah down a bit closer to his level. Her age and temperament made her easy prey for this sport of his.

Selah's doll-induced dreaminess was shattered by Skud's sudden appearance. She could not think of anything to say so just moved away to find Locenes. As she moved from the protective cover of the booth she caught a fresh sight of the Tolis and again stood gaping.

"Close yer mouth er I'll put somethin' in it," Skud taunted, "what's a matter with you?"

Selah's eyes next fell upon Rivoas in the cave and she began to point. "There he is!" she said, forgetting the vow of silence.

"What? What'er you pointin' at? You crazy?" Skud questioned.

"She's a nut cake, Skud. Let's get otta' here." Jojus shifted uneasily.

"It's the man, we have to follow!" Selah was gushing everything she had tried so hard to hold in.

By that time a couple more of Skud's boys had joined him.

"Fella's look at this here freak!" Skud joked, pointing at Selah.

Their little crowd now began to draw the attention of some surrounding adults.

Selah burst forth, "Skud, there is a man, a bright man who came to me and we have to escape with him through the cave, we have to go right away, there will be nothing left of Maraldia by the end of the festival!"

Now even Skud was getting uneasy. Some nearby adults began to question Selah. A few brushed it off as an overactive imagination while others thought there must be something wrong and moved closer to nab her. Selah sensed their intentions and squirmed away darting underneath a booth selling earthenware. Two men gave chase as Selah took refuge under a sheet covered table in one of the booths. When they lunged for her she bolted out knocking over a fortune in pottery and as the men pursued the entire booth collapsed. The infuriated booth owner now joined the chase but Selah had hidden in a candle booth several rows away. That booth met the same fate as Selah darted away to take her final refuge underneath a booth selling pastries. The whole square was now in an uproar and Locenes was in a panic.

Selah fleeing

"Selah! Selah!" The shouts of Locenes where drowned out in the overall tempest.

"Madam, is it your daughter we are searching for?" A policeman approached Locenes amidst the commotion, "The little girl with the strange babblings?"

Locenes suspected it was but replied, "I don't know, I only know my Selah is gone. She is seven years old, about this tall with brown hair." She held her hand at waist level.

"Sounds like one and the same," the policeman replied. "Please stay with me until we clear the square."

Locenes was sick from worry and from the accusatory eyes that met her as people were herded out of the square.

Once the square was clear Locenes walked through each row of booths calling out to Selah, "Selah! Selah! Please come out now! Everything is alright!"

But there was no reply.

"Look!" instructed one of the policemen, pointing to a small shock of hair sticking out from under the pastry table. The sleeping Selah had been found.

The walk to the police station at the corner of the square was thankfully a short one. However, the company inside was none too friendly, being made of angry merchants as well as adult witnesses. Once inside the usual protocol of police questioning and documentation was usurped by a curious Darrsce who happened by, having heard of the commotion.

"Well if it isn't the amusing little street girl from yesterday," Darrsce commented. "Sergeant, you can complete your paperwork later, please escort the girl with her mother and these witnesses into the council chambers. I'm sure the high council will be interested to know the reason for today's serious interruption in festival activities and the associated decrease in commerce," Darrsce directed.

Once before the council there was no hiding Selah's bizarre chatter. Talk of strange men in caves with doomsday predictions is not quickly forgotten and each witness told essentially the same story. Details of her remarkable vision and the bedroom visit where also dragged into the light.

Darrsce concluded the testimony by describing his encounter in the street the day before and deceitfully embellished it to suit his purpose, "In addition, I happen to know this family has some association with an explorer and merchant in our city who goes by the name of Noble, some of you may know him. I also know that Noble has been planning expeditions to the unexplored north. Do you think it coincidence that I saw this man that very morning on the same street? I would be last to assume the role of judge and jury but think we would be naïve to ignore these facts," then directing his words to the attending officers, "let us bring this man in for questioning."

Lered, who appeared distracted during the discussion finally spoke, "We will explore all details, Darrsce, including those related to Noble. A brigade will be sent to the mountain to determine the validity of the child's claims if only to silence speculators and a full physical examination of the child will be ordered soon enough. This situation is now under control and the investigators have our recommendations. We should allow them to complete their work. For now we have other matters to attend to."

Lered excused all except the council members and waited to hear the clicking of the latch on the other side of the great door.

"Gentlemen, please excuse my hurried manner on our previous topic, but I have just been informed that an armada of several hundred ships is moored in deep water just off our coast. We are not alone in the world."

6

In the council chambers the silence following Lered's announcement was full of disbelief. Everyone wished to speak at once yet no one could command his thoughts.

Lered summed it up for all stating, "Gentlemen, I scarcely know where to begin our discussion."

This introduction was enough impetus to loose a few tongues.

"I would think public security might be our first order of business," Councilman Ceresin suggested, always outspoken in his sincere concern for the people.

"Of course, practical matters first," Lered replied, reeling himself back from the brink of the philosophical, "but if this be an army bent on conquest I'm afraid the odds of a favorable outcome are remote."

"What do we know of these ships, how large and what configuration? Have men been seen?" Councilman Sapsion flooded the room with questions.

Sapsion was short and fit, a man of great energy. He was always the first to explore new ideas or begin new ventures.

"Men like us patrol the decks. They are not giants or beasts if that is what you mean. Their ships are too large for our small harbor and they are unlike any in Maraldia," Lered related. "I have already sent a contingent of 200 men to the shore several hours ago under the guise of training exercises. The ships are too distant for them to see unaided from the beach but our men are not stupid, they will guess the truth before long. We must manage this news properly to avoid a public panic."

"Then let us inform the public immediately with whatever we know," Ceresin suggested, "announce a civil address to be held tomorrow afternoon in the city square as with all matters of public importance. Openness will avoid the speculation which commonly fuels panic."

Little did the council know that just an hour ago as Selah began babbling to Skud about the end of Maraldia, a small delegation of "Freemen" were landing on their shores. The ranking Maraldian captain escorted the two visitors from the shore to the city center in a discrete covered carriage without police presence to avoid notice. As Ceresin finished his oratory a wide-eyed page entered the chamber in hurried form with a message for Lered. Whisperings and gestures were followed by his quick exit.

Lered stood, "Gentlemen, we have visitors."

The page returned momentarily with the announcement, "Your high council chair and esteemed council members, I give you Donem of the Freemen."

A chill gripped the spine of Lered as his eyes took in the form of Donem, and he suppressed a shiver.

Donem was a tall thin man with dark wavy hair, shoulder length. Though his face was weathered he had a certain handsome youthfulness to his appearance and was clean shaven. He wore loosely fitting pants which tucked in at the knee meeting high stockings there. A loose tunic of sorts covered his upper body, hip length and tied at the waist with a thick belt of leather and metal. Over all this he wore a full length cape of light material. And all was in black.

Donem bowed half a room away and touched one knee to the floor hands clasped tight to his breast as did his subordinate behind him. This gesture was unfamiliar to the Maraldians but they recognized it as a greeting of respect and reciprocated with the customary slight bow of the head and flowing half arm extension, palm up, which was their traditional welcome to a man of standing. Each sensed that Maraldian formalities did not apply to this occasion so one by one they exited their elevated seats and descended the few steps to the chamber floor. Polite introductions were made and Lered invited everyone to sit at the long petitioners table in the center of the room, equals all.

Lered put his initial ill feelings aside for the moment and began, "Most honored Donem, you can well imagine the state of mind in this council at present. When we awoke this morning our fair Maraldia was without question home to the most vast and civilized people in the world, indeed the only people in the world. In one instant that view has been shattered and we are feeling much smaller, given the size of your armada, than can be imagined. At the same time we are exhilarated for we are a people of exploration. We have a deep longing to find what lies beyond each ocean or mountain, though our means are meager. Your coming whets our appetite for all that we suspect the world has to offer which has remained beyond our grasp. Now I will not fill your ear with words any longer but wish to hear in full the purpose of your coming and all tidings you bring," then to Darrsce, "please instruct the page to bring the oldest and best wine he can find."

As Darrsce moved to the door, Donem relaxed a bit in his chair.

"I apologize for the concern our fleet must be raising in your people but I want to assure you that all has been intended for your great benefit. We are, after all, one and the same race, one and the same people. We are from a common ancestor. Allow me to explain."

At these words many of the councilmen tightened every muscle and leaned forward in their chairs a bit, so eager to hear Donem's words that they strained to fix every ounce of energy into the act of listening. Their pains were multiplied with the entrance of the page again who set before them, from some hidden basement vault, silver goblets unused for generations. Goblets, like festival ornaments, having the ancient stories carved in relief around the circumference. Lered noticed that Donem observed the images of the Givers with a wary eye and his uneasiness returned.

As the page exited, Donem continued, "My people, *our* people, are from across the southern ocean. We call ourselves the Freemen and our country is called simply enough Freeland. As you might expect we place high value on freedom for all, each man and clan. Freeland is a vast continent of incredible beauty and resources. We too are great explorers and have spread far and wide throughout the continent both east and west and to the far south. Our people have even settled across the great eastern ocean and founded Newfreeland more than 300 years ago. Here, we have brought gifts as a pledge of goodwill."

At this Donem's servant brought to the table a sack filled with numerous boxes. Donem opened the first and produced a small apparatus of wire and glass.

"See, my friends, the advancements of Freeland."

With this, Donem approached Ceresin, "May I?" he queried.

Ceresin nodded and Donem fixed the apparatus upon his face, glass pieces over the eyes and wires curling behind the ears. The expression on the face of Ceresin was enough to tell the story. The mouth of Ceresin fell embarrassingly open as he slowly rose from his chair wide eyed and gazing around the room.

"What is it, Ceresin?" Sapsion insisted, wishing that Donem had chosen him for this first experiment.

"It's astounding!" Ceresin gushed, "It's as though I can see for the first time!"

The crude apparatus roughly doubled the acuity of typical Maraldian vision. Selah would have wept to be reduced to this comparative level of blindness after receiving sight from Rivoas, though for all others it was an incredible improvement.

Several moments passed as the council took turns with the "oculars" as Donem called them. The room then quieted to excited whisperings as Donem, with a one sided smile, reached into another box and pulled from it what appeared to be a metal pipe with a handle affixed on one end. He then handed the box to his assistant and gave him a nod which sent him to the far end of the council chambers opposite the main entrance to prop the box against the wall. Donem retrieved the oculars and put them on his own face.

"Please move behind me for a moment," he requested of all as he raised the handled pipe to eye level with both arms straight in front of him.

The room fell deathly silent when, PANG! The sound of a thunderbolt ripped through the chamber and the pipe box leapt four paces into the air and across the room bounding back toward the councilmen, eventually coming to rest at the feet of Lered.

"What in the name of the Givers was that!" shouted Sapsion as the room erupted in panicked voices and questions.

The page burst through the door followed by several policemen, riot sticks in hand. The smell of burning sulfur hung in the air. Donem lowered the device and put it on the table as Lered picked up the metal box at his feet.

The room again fell silent as Donem explained, "Honorable Lered, see the iron ball now embedded in the back of the metal box? The impellor in my hand has projected the ball across the room with such force that it has become one with the rugged metal box and sent it sailing across the room to your feet. This

~ 65 ~

is but one use of the black powder we have invented in Freeland."

Donem smiled fully this time, delighted to be playing the magician. Fear and wonder filled the room as Lered excused the concerned intruders and settled the council back around the table amid murmurings and shufflings.

"These are astounding inventions Donem, things we have never imagined. Surely such wonders increase our hunger to learn all we can, but please continue with your history." Lered replaced Donem's gifts into their boxes as the now edgy council members regained their wits.

Donem continued, "Your Maraldia is a lost outpost of ours more than 5,000 years old. Though it has grown into a magnificent city it would be even more accurate to say it was an 'accidental' colony of Freeland. Your city is on the far northern frontier. There is no living thing more north than Maraldia."

Something twisted in the stomach of Lered, though he knew not why.

Donem continued, "By your own experience you can see that the terrain surrounding this place is inhospitable except on this isolated sliver of land which is protected by the great mountain from the brutal northern winds."

"The Tolis," interjected Sapsion.

"Is that the name you have given to the mountain? We have called it Boundary Peak since it serves as such for all creatures with the breath of life. Then yes, the Tolis. To say accidental is no insult to your great people. Your ancestors are our ancestors. In their explorations our fathers ventured north to this place stopping for fresh water from the river."

"The Elif," again from Sapsion.

"As you please. None the less our history records that their excursion was cut short by the wicked northern winds. Storms tore apart their ships, 25 in all. The storm took its daily toll of life for a full month, driving the retreating wounded fleet across the ocean and dragging one ship after another into the depths. In the end only three sailors returned to Freeland in a small lifeboat and then only by the best of good fortune. They were little better than mad men when they returned, though our fathers did glean from them the account I have just put before you. Stories grew as the years passed that some were left on that far northern shore near the great mountain as the ships were being driven, but there were also stories of dragons and sea nymphs pulling the ships into oblivion so all such tales were assigned the status of myth."

Lered's uneasiness had only increased as Donem's dialog progressed. He could not refute the account of Maraldia's beginnings, but the history left him wanting.

At this point the page returned with a crate of dusty bottles. Lered pulled one from the mix noting it was older than himself and opened it with his knife, always at the ready. He served each one and proposed a toast, "To expanding horizons," and was met with tinkling goblets and "Here! Here!" all around. The council members were filled with heady emotion and the dusty spirits enhanced that feeling. Donem would not touch his carved goblet, and Lered took note.

Donem continued, "One thing was certain to our ancestors, the northern frontier was henceforth closed to all but fools."

"Yet here you sit with hundreds of ships," Darrsce's words betrayed his skepticism.

Donem slowly looked toward Darrsce and replied with a drawn-out, "Yeeees," then continued, "four years ago we found the remains of a ship washed up on our shores. We knew from the construction that it was none of ours and we knew from the currents that it came from the north."

"So the ancient myths gained new life," Lered interjected.

"Indeed they did," said Donem. "The following year three scout ships were sent with fear and trepidation on a northern expedition and with not a little fanfare. Their mission was to locate the mythical city you call your home. This expedition came within a few miles of your shore just two years ago and saw the form of the giant Tolis and your great city in the distance through ocuscopes --- something like the ocular that I have demonstrated, only much more powerful. Unfortunately the small fleet was forced to make a hasty retreat as the winds increased. Indeed, one of the ships was lost though all men returned safely aboard the other two. The people of Freeland were greatly energized by the report and commissioned the armada you see along your coast. We have come to offer any who wish free passage back to Freeland and a homestead in our country along with it. You are our brothers, long ago forgotten, and we wish to offer a reunion if it is acceptable."

The council was astonished at the prospect, such an enormous proposition.

Darrsce spoke what had already occurred to most of them, "But why so many ships on this first visit? Why a gigantic armada as a first contact?"

Donem responded as though he had anticipated the question, "My dear Darrsce, our people are adept at seafaring and have spread throughout the entire habitable world. But our expertise also gives us great respect and fear of this northern frontier. We have planned well for this one foray into these regions and put all our energies into the mission, but it is not without some concern. We cannot guarantee that there will be another attempt."

"Are you saying that this gracious offer is extended now and never again?" Darrsce replied, smelling something peculiar.

Donem was calm, "It cannot be guaranteed. If our return is successful perhaps there will be further opportunities. However, as I have told you we have never had a completely successful return. We have come at great risk to the life and treasure of our nation, come as a gesture of goodwill but the moods of the people can be fickle. Today, Maraldia captivates the imagination of all Freeland and the people have invested in a vast armada with a bold mission. Tomorrow there will be other matters of concern. Surely as a high councilman you understand the ebb and flow of public interest." Donem leaned back with a slight left tilt of the head to address Darrsce.

"Certainly," Darrsce conceded, eager to be placated.

"May we come aboard and familiarize ourselves with your ships, learn all we can about your proposal before meeting with the people tomorrow evening?" Lered questioned.

"At your earliest convenience," Donem replied.

"Then let the notices be posted. A meeting in the city square tomorrow one hour before sundown with councilmen dispatched to each of the four corners of the city to deliver the same message," Lered commanded.

Donem added, "I applaud your expediency Chairmen Lered. There is in fact the utmost need for haste. You see our northward journey to Maraldia was not without incident and took weeks longer than expected. We only have days now before the winter winds begin their descent upon us and with so large a fleet I am not willing to press my luck. All who wish to reunite with their ancient countrymen will need to be on board before the end of the festival."

"This is too sudden! The people need time! This council needs time!" Sapsion spoke for them all as the entire council erupted in murmurings and objections.

Donem arose and swept his coat tails behind him.

"Great adventures are never without great sacrifice. The offer is before you. History will record these days as epic. Seize them if you will or shrink away."

Donem's challenge inspired some and irritated others.

Lered weighed it all and spoke evenly, "Even the heroic chew well before they swallow. We will proceed with all good speed and rational consideration. For now please allow us to show you a bit of hospitality. Pageboy, show Donem to our best quarters overlooking the square."

Darrsce was among the inspired and sidled up to Donem as he moved to the door, "May I have a word with you in private? I will come to your quarters in half an hour if it is agreeable."

Here was the chance Darrsce had been waiting for. What better opportunity would ever come to surpass even the greatest business exploits of his loveless father?

"It would be my pleasure."

Donem locked eyes with Darrsce and there was a knowing that passed between them as with those who share a secret.

"My pleasure indeed."

After being released from the council chambers, Locenes took Selah home. All the way Locenes felt like the eyes of the city were on her though, in fact, those who could identify them as instigators were few and the sensation was mostly imaginary.

"Momma, why doesn't everyone believe me? I would never tell a lie."

Selah's question was full of sadness.

Locenes paused before answering. She just wished to sleep or hide, anything to make the dread of unfriendly investigations into her private affairs go away. But it was too late for that and if Selah's story was accurate a return to normal would never come.

"It is a strange story, Selah, like none ever told before. It demands a response and most people do not take kindly to demands," Locenes explained.

Arriving home late that morning Locenes and Selah felt as if they had already been through an entire day's hard labor. After grabbing some leftover flat cakes and milk they fell fast asleep spooning together on Selah's bed. Selah dreamed of distant sights and Locenes dreamed of Selah. Several hours later they were awakened by the noisy entrance of Keeres.

"Thank you very much old friend!" they could hear Keeres say in grateful tones.

Before he could hang his coat both were up and at his side.

"Papa!" Selah welcomed, burying her face in his hip while Locenes gave him a peck on the lips.

~ 71 ~

"I understand you two have had an eventful day," Keeres spoke with some untold knowing and a raised eyebrow.

"Word travels quickly in our small city…what time is it?" Locenes questioned.

"Midafternoon," Keeres answered, moving to the kitchen for the last bit of flatbread.

"Yes, I've heard about your morning though I'd be pleased to hear it afresh from you. I've also been told that the brigade of police sent to the base of the mountain found nothing though my suspicion is that none of them took the task very seriously. They probably spent more time tipping an ale than looking for mysterious men in caves."

Keeres' conclusions were based partly on conjecture and partly on the smell of the police officer's breath he had been speaking with just as he entered the house.

"Oh Papa, can we please go to the man, to Rivoas?" Selah pleaded with a fervor born of fresh rest. "I can see what the police can't and I hate Maraldian ale!"

Keeres and Locenes exchanged glances and nods. Within 15 minutes father and daughter had packed a few items and set off for the mountain leaving Locenes to attend to the home and receive any news that might come.

It only took them 30 minutes to negotiate the city streets and reach the edge of the forest, Keeres carrying Selah most of the way on his shoulders in order to keep an adult pace. They entered the forest footpath and edged closer to the Tolis.

"Papa, he is happy to see us coming!" Selah bubbled, "He is smiling at us."

Keeres was a little uncomfortable with the idea of being seen without being able to see. The reality of Rivoas was beginning to take hold of him.

"Indeed," he replied, "in which direction should I direct my fabulous smile? I should like to return the sentiment." Keeres played with her.

"Over there."

Selah pointed slightly left of the path and just above the trees. Keeres summoned up his best toothy grin and flashed it in the direction Selah had indicated.

"You made him laugh!" Selah chuckled, "He is laughing at your funny face."

In truth, Keeres thought he heard something that sounded a bit like a laugh. Or did he feel it? He wasn't sure.

The path had now come to an end and there was nothing but thick trees all in full color. They stopped for a moment and Selah climbed down.

"This way, Papa, he is pointing this way."

Selah began navigating, alternately watching her step and peering around trees and branches for a sight of Rivoas. Keeres followed his little girl for 30 minutes in this fashion before coming to a small clearing with a very old tree on the southern edge away from the Tolis. The trunk of the tree was far thicker than the rest in the forest and would have taken eight or nine adults arms spread and holding hands to encircle it. In fact, Keeres could not remember ever seeing another like it. Limbs extending upward from its massive trunk began only a bit above his head and were thick enough to be stout trees on their own. These were short, however, and the subsequently thinner and thinner offshoots resulted in a tree no higher than any other of the forest. A massive bull of a tree it was.

"So where to now?" queried Keeres, seeing Selah's gaze fixed upward.

"He is sitting down. Maybe he wants us to rest. He was pointing before but now he is sitting," Selah explained, trying to act the part of a leader for her comparatively blind father.

"I don't need a rest," Keeres showed a slight impatience, "we do not have an abundance of time before nightfall and I'd prefer to be out of these woods by then. Maybe we should just go search the base of the mountain, it must not be more than a few hundred paces from here."

Keeres flashed a forced smile toward the mountain in the direction Selah was gazing but felt no laughter in his bones this time. Instead, an almost imperceptible twinge of shame ran through him and he retreated under the shade of the big tree and sat down.

Selah sat in view of the mountain cave cross legged just under the outer edge of the tree's enormous canopy, alternately glancing between the mountain and her father.

As they sat a bit uneasy, a gray squirrel darted out of a hole at the base of the tree where the trunk and roots and soil all became one. He scampered out a little farther than Selah and stood on his hind legs head cocked to one side whiskers twitching, looking at her. He then quickly scampered back into his hole at the base of the tree. This happened again a moment later. Then again. Then again. Selah and Keeres were beginning to have good fun with this performance when Keeres decided to see what would happen if he surprised the squirrel at the entrance to his hole. As he approached, his creeping silence suddenly gave way to a tumult of cracking roots and crashing soil!

"Ahhhh!" Keeres was gone, swallowed by the hungry ground!

"Papa!"

Selah shouted and rushed to the spot of his disappearance, though a bit too hastily, for there was more unstable soil all around the spot.

"Papa!"

Selah shouted as she tumbled in the hole as well. Keeres saw it coming and broke her fall as best he could. They both found themselves a pace or two underground covered in dirt and debris. Selah lay by his side brushing the dirt and moss from her face.

"Selah, are you all right?" Keeres spoke as he evaluated his own wellbeing.

"I'm all right, Papa, but Mommy will be very mad about my new trousers."

Keeres hugged her and they both glanced up to the sight of the gray squirrel on the edge of their newly formed hole, standing on his hind legs head cocked and whiskers twitching in usual manner. Keeres thought he could feel that unusual laughter again and it buoyed his spirits.

Selah tumbling in

After a moment's reorientation, Keeres and Selah realized they had fallen on the landing of a set of hard clay stairs leading downward into the ground. From this landing Keeres hoisted Selah above ground to look for the face for Rivoas who was now standing.

"He's not doing anything, Papa, just standing there," Selah puzzled.

"Well, either he led us to this tree with a hidden cavern to bury us alive or he wanted us to find these steps," Keeres conjectured.

Keeres' Maraldian sense of adventure was now getting into high gear and he began clearing away more of the sinking soil and roots that spanned away in the direction of the underground stairway. It was clear that this entrance was once reinforced with wooden walls and roof which had long ago decayed.

When he had cleared enough to provide himself sufficient headroom on the quickly descending staircase he spoke, "Well my dear Selah, I believe we have gone as far as we can for today. I have no torch to light the way. We will need to return tomorrow."

There was a measure of disappointment in Keeres' words and in Selah's expression. Both felt that something very desirable was only a handbreadth away and to stop now was like pulling the cake away after a single stolen lick of frosting. Yet both knew it wiser to tackle this expedition with more daylight and the needed supplies than the fast approaching sunset would now allow.

Keeres and Selah covered the opening as best they could with branches and leaves and headed back home with the smile of Rivoas upon their backs.

That half an hour seemed like half a day to Darrsce as he waited to seek out Donem in his quarters. Darrsce had always been keen to sniff out opportunity while others were preoccupied with matters of duty or conscience. He approached the door using every ounce of energy to appear casual, though his mind raced like a youth interviewing for an apprenticeship with a master craftsmen. Should he tap loudly or softly upon the door? Slowly or with rapid cadence? He did not have to decide.

"Darrsce, my friend!" Donem greeted from behind as Darrsce stood in the doorway, "Come in please. I've just finished a pleasant visit with Council Chair Lered. He is a wise man indeed, understandably circumspect."

Darrsce was a bit ruffled at being second in line for a personal interview and cursed himself for not following Donem back to his quarters immediately. Who knows what ideas might now be rendered impotent due to Lered's influence.

"Yes of course, thank you." Darrsce entered first.

The boxes containing the oculars and the impellor sat on the desk. The closed window directly across the room faced north upon the square and let in the setting western sun, casting orange light through the doorway to the right which led to the sleeping quarters. Though he had been a council member working in this building for years, Darrsce had never been into these privileged quarters. The walls were dark stained oak, with carved vertical beams all around every two paces or so. Pictures of historic councils, men of ancient renown and an occasional outdoor panorama decorated the walls. Donem slipped past Darrsce and found his place on an antique sofa, crossed his legs and pulled from his pocket a small pipe of sorts. It was thin and straight with no bowl, just a small hole along its length on one end, into which Donem stuffed a mix of dried leaves. He ignited this mixture with another device which Darrsce had never seen. It produced a small flame which he held to one end of the pipe while sucking through the opposite end. He relaxed and invited Darrsce, who had been surveying the scene from the doorway, to join him.

"Come, Darrsce," he motioned to the cushioned wooden chair perpendicular to the sofa, "do you smoke?"

"No, thank you."

Darrsce feigned knowledge though the practice of inhaling the vapors of burning dried leaves was wholly unknown to the Maraldians. The sight of Donem blowing smoke through his nose and mouth added a strange intrigue to the encounter, as though Darrsce were holding council with a fire breathing beast from another planet altogether.

Darrsce took his assigned seat. "But I am not," he began.

"Say again?" Donem queried, not catching the meaning.

"Understandably circumspect."

Darrsce shifted his chair slightly to face Donem more directly.

"Ah yes, Lered. It is a good quality in the normal ebb and flow of events. But these are not normal events, eh Darrsce? In such times as this it is beneficial to have a leader with a highly developed sense of intuition."

Donem blew smoke out of the left side of his mouth to avoid Darrsce, though he looked him directly in the eye.

"So what does that make you?" Donem was getting to the point.

"A pioneer if you will. Though for centuries my family has been among those leading Maraldia in business, my passion is more creative and progressive," Darrsce measured his words, edging in toward his business.

"Both business and governments would benefit greatly from creative and progressive leaders," Donem returned, squinting down at his pipe.

"Yes, I like to think I have brought those elements to the council, though it is a maddeningly traditional group on the whole. I fight to exhaustion for the slightest progress in this city," Darrsce bemoaned.

"Such as?" Donem queried.

"Such as a measure I proposed only last month to remove ancient restrictions on behaviors I consider to be individual and private matters," Darrsce explained.

"Ah, you place exceptionally high value on personal freedom."

Donem tracked along, smiling as one who has found a kindred spirit.

"Indeed, though such inherent rights are blatantly obvious to me these ideas are opaque as the Tolis for the council. Lered in particular opposes me at every turn."

Darrsce's face went sour for a moment and it did not escape the notice of Donem. Darrsce sensed he may be sharing too much and moved the conversation back to his original intent.

"But the council work is really of secondary interest to me. My first love is exploration. You can see why your appearance is of special interest to me," Darrsce chose his words carefully, not wishing to appear as a beggar seeking favors in the new world of Freeland.

"Go on." Donem was blasé.

"Tell me, Donem, what do you know of the regions north of Maraldia?" Darrsce hinted at his potentially valuable secret, wishing to bolster his position as an equal to Donem with his expansive claims.

Donem stiffened almost imperceptibly, though Darrsce did perceive it.

"I expect that there is nothing to the north of these mountains but the dead bodies of brave and foolish explorers."

Donem just as quickly regained his casual attitude, "Certainly you know these winters better than I, and I know enough."

"And what if I told you I have evidence to the contrary?" countered Darrsce, playing the cards he had. However, his recent discoveries seemed paltry and speculative compared with the fire breathing flesh and blood a few paces away from him.

"I'd say it should appear very interesting indeed to a man such as you were a day ago, locked tightly into a very limited sphere," Donem downplayed.

"And what manner of man am I today?" Darrsce inquired, already knowing what to expect in reply.

"A man whose prospects have multiplied a thousand times over I suppose. But make what you will of your situation; I perceive you are an intelligent man."

Donem was again smug in his position as generous benefactor.

There was a moment of silence between the two as Donem gave attention to his spent pipe and Darrsce glanced out the window to the north.

"So what of these multiplied prospects?" Darrsce paused and began again more along the pretense of the selfless leader, "What can *I* do to make this reunification an unmitigated success for all of our peoples?"

Donem read Darrsce's true intentions and after a moment spoke more slowly than before, "Make no mistake, my dear Darrsce, there is plenty of room for creative and progressive leadership in Freeland. Especially those who wish to throw off all fetters of tradition and ancient superstition. Maraldian leaders who are instrumental in this migration will most surely gain high standing in our great nation. As a long standing leader of Maraldia you are in a unique position at this crucial time, when hopes…" he paused for effect, "*and* fears are high, to provide calm and clear direction to your people."

"Forgive my boldness, Donem. I have significant standing here in Maraldia, small though it is by comparison to Freeland. It is more than most could wish for. What assurances may I expect of improved position in Freeland? Only a fool takes on risk without measuring the probability of significant reward."

Darrsce stood and circled around the back of his chair and stepped to the window, all pretense of the selfless leader now shattered.

Donem sensed a chance for checkmate, "But 'your first love is exploration', you have said it yourself. What would such a man do in a city depleted of most of its population, hemmed in on all sides by these furious winters and nagged by the thought of what might have been? Plan hopeless expeditions to the north? He would soon be little better than a mad man."

Donem pressed the reality of the situation hard upon Darrsce.

Donem continued, "And as for a reward commensurate to the risk I can only say that explorers are accustomed to such uncertainties, though I will paint you this picture; I have already attained significant position among my people, my presence here as an ambassador testifies to that fact. If this venture is a success it will go even better with me in Freeland. Those who work with me to accomplish it will have proved themselves and rise with me in Freeland. It is only smart business to maintain alliances among successful partners."

Donem stood and followed the lead of Darrsce, circling the sofa and took a step toward the window. He knew his words would marinate best immersed in silence, and said no more as he approached.

Darrsce stood looking out at the Tolis. His true situation was for the first time becoming clear to him. Looking out the window to the north he thought to himself:

The old Maraldia will in very short order be gone forever. Who knows what will remain? Will there be enough people left to reestablish a working society? Will any recognize my long held authority? Will those left descend into looting and barbarism? The coming of the Freemen does not leave the status quo as a viable option for a man like me.

He surveyed the busy square and the houses sheltered in the shade of the mountain while silence hung in the oaken room.

Darrsce quickly turned from the northern exposure of the window to look Donem square in the eye, "Then let us begin."

By the time Noble was found and brought into the station Darrsce had already instructed the Chief of Police to detain him as long as possible pending further statements from family, investigation of the girl's claims, and whatever procedural nonsense that could be trumped up. Unfortunately for Noble, festival related police work would provide ample excuse for delayed proceedings. Noble was escorted unceremoniously into a minimum security cell, a bare straw stuffed mattress on the floor and rough wooden stool in the corner.

As the sun disappeared beneath the western Maraldian skyline, Keeres and Selah arrived home. Before they could utter a word of their incredible story, Locenes filled their ears with the news of Noble's arrest. Remembering the accusations of Darrsce earlier that day, Locenes had inquired through friends at the station and learned of his arrest only an hour earlier.

Selah's heart pounded at the thought of poor Noble sitting in a cold jail because of something she had done.

"Papa, we have to see Noble and bring him some pies or cakes!" Selah always associated treats with comfort.

After refreshing themselves, they quickly packed some hard rolls and cheese and headed off to the station, all three of them. The walk was filled with discussion of the underground stairs and the laugh of Rivoas and what it all might lead to.

"Lieutenant, we are here to see Noble," Keeres announced to the man behind the desk.

With a squinty eye the Lieutenant surveyed the three. After checking their packs he led them through a narrow metal doorway behind and to the right of the desk, "This way," he motioned and followed them in, "all the way to the end."

Noble's was the last in a series of five cells, all empty save his.

"Brother Noble!" Keeres reached his hand through the bars.

"Brother Keeres." Noble clasped it firmly and gave a hint of a smile.

"Noble!"

Selah reached through the bars but was only able to manage an awkward hip hug due to her short reach and the interfering bars.

"I'm sorry, I'm sure I've been a bad girl," tears welling up in her eyes, "we brought you some cheese."

"Ha!" Noble rejoined, grinning at Keeres and Locenes. "A good cheese can make a man forget almost any misfortune. And I'm sure if all men were as *bad* as you, Selah, Maraldia would be a much better place."

Selah wasn't sure what he meant but could tell by his smile that he wasn't angry with her.

"Please, refresh yourself," said Keeres as he handed Noble a skin of water and a parcel of cheese.

Keeres continued, "We are sorry to be in any way responsible for your current situation. Frankly it is something of a puzzle as to why we are."

Locenes interrupted, which was unlike her, "Darrsce has somehow made a connection between Selah's strange talk and you. He claims to have seen you in the street yesterday morning when, sorry to say, we had another small commotion with Selah. He must have been a passerby. We were only in the street for a moment…he must have been there."

"But I surely was not," Noble reached for some water from Keeres, "I was in my shop from before sunrise to past midday."

"Then Darrsce is mistaken, or worse," Keeres returned quickly.

Noble added, "Darrsce is not favorably disposed to me in any case, my friends. As you well know he has a few stores of his own and has offered to buy my enterprise outright. Of course I could not sell, it is my heart and soul. Since my refusal he has more than once stopped by to inform me I would soon be out of business."

After a moment Noble continued, "But please, whether or not Darrsce is looking for a reason to close my shop is one thing. Men are never short on schemes to undo one another. My chief concern is with this talk of a raving mad little girl."

Noble gave a reassuring wink to Selah that provoked a shy cheesy grin, then finished his thought, "Now you bring news of prior public commotions with my little friend. I have seen madness in men but never in a sweet child such as Selah. I'm afraid there is more to this tale than you let on. I do not deserve to know another family's secrets but at least reassure me that Selah is as innocent as ever."

Selah looked up at Noble with wide happy eyes softly munching some of the cheese meant for him.

Keeres and Locenes glanced at each other, and Selah looked as though she would burst if not allowed to tell her friend the entire story. There was a moment of silence between them and then Keeres spoke, "She is the sanest among us, I am sure. And yes, there is much more to our story which by the glances of my ladies here I think we are about to fill your ears with."

Noble pulled up the rough stool inside the cell indicating that he was ready while Keeres dragged over a rough wooden bench from across the narrow hall. The three of them took turns walking Noble through the details of Selah's visit from Rivoas and his command to escape north and the sign given of her astounding vision. They discussed their afternoon's adventure to the underground stairs and Keeres even told of the information he had received from Rohon about the mysterious ships and the markings there which mirrored those on the old festival ornaments, details he had not even shared with Locenes or Selah yet. Finally, Keeres told the story of finding Selah at the wall amidst the dead wolves, including the opposition of Darrsce at the council...a story new to Selah herself.

They all sat quietly for a moment until Locenes interjected, "Keeres, did you see the posting outside the station as we walked in? It announced a public meeting tomorrow evening in the square, as well as in each corner of the city?"

"No, I suppose I was too preoccupied to notice. What else did it say?"

"Nothing, just a proclamation of the meeting by order of the high council."

"There has not been a public meeting of that sort since the last council chair died and Lered was appointed. Has something happened to Lered?" Noble's question was rhetorical.

"It is very unusual for such a public meeting to be called during the week of the festival, very disruptive to the merchants," Keeres mused, looking down at his boots, still soiled with the moss from the hidden stairway.

Just then the Lieutenant wrenched open the metal door with a loud clang, "That's enough, let's go!"

Noble hurriedly finished, "Keeres please look under the rain barrel near the rear entrance to my shop. Lift the triangular paving stone and there you will find keys to the front entrance. Take what you need for your journey and find out where those stairs lead. I trust Selah more than I trust the council these days. May the speed of the north wind be with you."

The crescent moon was just rising as the three of them left the police station. Selah said nothing but as they walked home she could see a small fire burning in the cave in the mountain and the shadow of the one sitting by it.

10

Keeres and Selah had no idea that their excursion to the secret stairs had been watched step by step and move by move. Skud had seen them set out and having nothing better to do, loitered along behind at a safe distance and once in the woods stealthily tracked them. A member of Skud's raggedy gang was with him, Kwea, who was 15 years older than the rest and a head taller. Kwea fit in nicely with Skud's gang. He was terribly dull of mind, sometimes even delusional, but had found a family in the juvenile band because he could provide them useful service. He could mingle in adult circles without drawing too much attention (provided he kept his mouth shut) and bring back useful information, information which might help the gang in their petty raids and thievery. He could also purchase ale and tobacco without anyone batting an eyelash. In this way Kwea earned his keep among the brotherhood.

"You kin come as long as ya don't make a single sound, ya hairy beast," Skud insulted Kwea into submission. Kwea was in fact a hairy fellow, dark beard reaching to his chest.

"Yes, yes!" were the last words Kwea spoke for the next hour. He had learned long ago that things went better if he kept quiet and more or less followed the leading of the gang.

It was easy enough to avoid notice while in the city streets, following at a distance only limited by his poor vision, but quite another matter in the quiet woods. As Keeres and Selah entered the woodsy path, Skud and Kwea carefully cut their own parallel trail through thick foliage about 30 paces behind and 30 paces to the east on the very fringe of his Maraldian vision. It was fortunate for him that Selah, whose keen eyes could have spotted him like he was at arm's length, was completely preoccupied with Rivoas and watching her own step. Otherwise their escapade would be over. Kwea mirrored every contorted move of Skud, stepping only where he stepped and mimicking every quiet twisting move through mangled branches. Their going was slow and at one point they lost sight of Keeres and Selah altogether, only finding them again after listening carefully for their voices. When Skud finally had them again in his sights they were resting beneath the great tree. Skud marveled at the tree and wondered why he had never sought out these woods before as a refuge for his gang.

Skud felt a pokey finger in his back.

"What?!" Skud's whisper had the effect of a shout upon Kwea who withered and pointed at Keeres and Selah.

"They ain't doing nothin' Kwea, just jokin' about some squirrel!" he again shout-whispered, but before he could finish Keeres had tumbled into the underground stairway.

Kwea's eyes went wide which ended Skud's abuse and refocused his attention again to the tree. There he saw Selah disappear into the ground and poke her head up a moment later like a gopher coming out of a hole. They watched as Keeres pulled away more of the loose soil and subsequently recovered the opening with branches and leaves. They watched them excitedly leave the way they came.

When Keeres and Selah were a safe distance away, Skud more noisily pushed through the forest between him and the marvelous tree. Again the pokey finger.

"What?!" Skud scolded, this time with some real volume.

Kwea looked intently at Skud with wide eyes and pointed carefully at his own pursed lips.

"Talk if ya haf to," Skud directed as he turned away to look at the edges of the hole now covered with branches.

"I were's real good, weren't I Skud? I were's real quiet, just like you said!" Kwea was excited to highlight his accomplishment.

"Quiet enough. Now help me pull some o' these branches away. Let's take a look at what they stumbled into. Maybe some buried treasure!" Skud imagined a fortune big enough to deliver him from Stohl.

They worked quickly and hopped down to the landing of the stairway.

"Just dirt." Kwea surmised, tugging his beard with disappointment.

Skud did not answer but started rustling through the pack he always carried slung across his back. He pulled out the small bottle of hard liquor he always carried, his best friend when times were worst.

"Can I git a swig?" Kwea interjected.

"Gim'me your shirt," Skud demanded, ignoring the request.

"I'll be cold Skud," Kwea pleaded.

"Fine, just stand still," Skud directed.

Skud produced a knife.

"Ohhhhh," Kwea cowered.

Skud cut off Kwea's shirt around the middle leaving him shoulders and upper torso only.

"Ohhhh, Skud, I'm in a bad way Skud," Kwea sorrowed over his loss, looking down at his half shirt.

Skud soaked the cloth in the spirits and dug through his pack for a small piece of iron and a flint. He tied the soaked rag in a balled up fashion to one of the nearby sticks and immediately began striking the iron and flint to produce sparks. After what seemed like a long time to them both, Skud was able to get his torch lit to the great delight of Kwea.

"Hahooo! Kin you make me one, Skud?!" Kwea blurted, forgetting for a moment that this one cost him his shirt.

"This one's enough. There might still be somethin' worth gittin' in this tunnel. Let's go." Skud instructed, starting down the stairs.

"Can I hold it?"

Kwea fixated on the blue and yellow flame but Skud was already three steps down and going further. Kwea quickly followed not wanting to be left behind.

Skud and Kwea in the cave

The passageway quickly narrowed, becoming only wide enough for one at a time. The walls transitioned from dirt and clay into rock as they descended. The ceiling was surprisingly high, high enough for even Kwea to stand upright and barely touch it standing on his tip toes. The path leveled out after about 30 steps down and led straight, as far as Skud could tell, toward the Tolis. After maybe 300 paces Skud began to get worried.

"Crawlin' around under the ground is one thing Kwea but crawlin' around under a mountain is another," Skud vocalized his apprehension.

"Another what, Skud?" Kwea was more or less oblivious and therefore braver.

"Might as well be talkin' to a gopher," Skud mumbled under his breath but kept walking as the path started to slant upward. "and this torch ain't gonna last forever."

The path began sloping steeper upward and following a switchback pattern every 40 paces or so. Skud had seen these winding walkways in pictures of mountain trails. Just as he was about to give up and turn back he noticed a faint light reflecting off the stone wall of the next upcoming switchback curve.

"Quiet Kwea. Real quiet now," Skud instructed.

Skud's anticipation was showing. He quickly snuffed out the torch and felt the quivering hands of Kwea grab his shoulders. Now that the torch was out he began to smell a sweet fragrance like that of a garden coming at them in a faint breeze from above. They crept quietly as mice the rest of the way to the next switchback corner, the faint reflected light now seemed almost like dawn. As Skud edged around the last corner another hand came out of that emerging dawn and rested on his shoulder.

"Welcome!" came the deep smooth voice as Skud melted into a pure faint.

11

Keeres and Selah set out before daybreak for Noble's shop. It was now the third day of the festival and the usual predawn buzz associated with festival preparations was unusually quiet.

"Papa, there is no fire in the mountain cave and it is too dark to see anything without it," Selah fretted. She had come to feel something of a bond with Rivoas and was uncomfortable when she could not see him.

"Don't worry, darling, it will be daylight by the time we make it to the woods," Keeres' words comforted the child.

They found the keys just as Noble had instructed, though the lack of a lamp made it more difficult than you might expect. They entered the shop and found the needed packs, lamps, oil, flint and a knife or two. They grabbed a small canvas and some rope, more items than they really needed, but the uncertainty of it all made Keeres cautious.

"Papa, look. Do we need any of these?"

Selah had wandered into the section of the shop devoted to hunting supplies, bows and arrows of every shape and size. There were also swords and hatchets.

"I don't expect we'll need any of those for now," Keeres spoke thoughtfully making a mental note that these could be useful in uncertain times and such times may not be too distant if Rivoas was a man of truth, if he is a man at all.

The walk back to the big tree seemed faster than yesterday as all trips do once the destination is known. The sun had now risen and Selah could see Rivoas in his usual spot, though he was not looking at her and seemed otherwise engaged.

"Someone or something has gone in ahead of us," Keeres spoke as they both noticed the open hole at the same time.

"Papa, what if it's a wild animal and it's angry! We should have brought the arrows!" Selah worried.

"I don't think so, I see human footprints on the landing."

Keeres lowered his pack down and just for good measure gave a quick glance for beasts before jumping in himself. Though he found none, he couldn't help regret not bringing a sword. He lit two lamps before reaching up for Selah.

"Here is a small lamp for you," he held it out to Selah, "be careful of the hot glass. Stick close behind."

Selah took it and an excited sudden shiver ran through her. In all her hours of imaginary adventures none ever included underground caves. She wondered if Noble had ever adventured underground and was excited at the idea of telling him a great story like the ones he had always shared with her.

Before she had a chance to dwell long on this, Keeres was calling, "Come now, darling, be careful on these steps."

Keeres descended the 30 steps quickly and noticed something that Skud had missed.

"Selah, do you see these writings on the wall?"

He held the lamp close to the granite and ran his fingers over the etchings.

"It looks like something of a crude map. This part looks like it represents the Tolis, this large hump here," Keeres motioned as he spoke.

"And this part looks like the Great Ocean because there are ships on it," Selah replied. She was proud to be participating so fully in the discovery.

"Yes, if that is the Ocean as you say and this represents the Tolis and these edges the wild forests," he was pointing and gesturing at this map of his entire known world, "then what are these markings beyond the mountain?"

"It looks like a chair with a great sun behind it," Selah spoke what she saw.

"A very grand chair indeed. See this crown around the top of the high back?" Keeres brushed away a bit of moss that had grown over the etching.

"It is," Selah's voice was full of wonder, "but there is nothing beyond the Tolis and the northern tundra right Papa?"

Keeres looked at her but did not speak. A lump rose in his throat and he was afraid that any words would come out cracked and broken. He did not need to speak because Selah answered her own question.

"Rivoas wants us to follow this line right here, Papa, through the mountain toward the big chair. We are at the start of the line right here."

The warm softness of her little finger was contrasted against the cold rigid granite.

"Let's go," was all that Keeres could manage and he started through the tunnel.

Keeres knew from the wall map that the switchbacks lay ahead, so he was not surprised when the gradient of the trail edged upward. By the time they reached the last bend, Keeres was breathing a bit hard not because of the difficulty of the climb but at the thought that what, up to now, had only been his child's fantasy was about to look him directly in the eye. For him it was the anticipation of first contact with another world. Selah, however, displayed the same kind of innocent delight she always did, as though peering into the oven at a batch of fresh muffins just fully baked.

Keeres turned the last corner from which daylight was now streaming in. Transitioning from the lamplight to the brightness of the sun blinded him for a moment but he could just make out the outline of a tall figure. The lump again returned to his throat and he maneuvered into a position which took the backlighting of the rising sun away from the stranger, the cave wall now in the background. His eyes quickly adjusted and the face before him came into focus.

Kwea.

"Hi, Mr. Kwea!" Selah spoke first.

Selah had always liked Kwea because, in spite of being in Skud's gang, Kwea always treated Selah nicely. Skud's lessons in cruelty had never driven that natural tendency from him.

"Hi, little Selah! We seen you comin' even before you got into the woods!" Kwea welcomed, feeling proud to be entertaining guests. Apparently Kwea's vision was now as good as Selah's and he was eager to talk about it.

"So, those were *your* footprints in the cave," Keeres surmised aloud.

All of the welled up emotion he was feeling had been drained away at the sight of Kwea and he was back to a purely Maraldian worldview, but only for a moment.

"Welcome, Keeres!" came the deep smooth voice that had sent Skud to his knees the night before.

Keeres turned slowly to the sight of the most alive face he had ever seen. He remembered Selah describing him as "bright" but not really in the sense of lightness. Now he understood what she meant as he looked into the eyes of Rivoas. It was as if by comparison everything around him was out of focus. In reality it was Rivoas that was somehow in super focus. Keeres instinctively held out his hand and Rivoas grabbed it with both of his, giving it a firm, short shake. Keeres felt a peace come over him that he had not known since the days of sleeping in his mother's arms.

"And welcome to you Selah, my child. You have done well and you shall do even better," Rivoas smiled as he spoke, crouching down to look Selah directly in the face.

Rivoas wore the same robes Selah remembered from only a few nights ago, a deep green lightweight material draped to the ground with arms fuller than needed and a broad hood now folded away to the back. A leather belt pulled in at the waist and joined a leather sash in the front, looping over the shoulder to the back and holding a small quiver with half a dozen arrows. He was barefoot with straight black hair a bit less than shoulder length and pulled back without a part. An intricate lightweight silver band with seven interwoven strands circled his head, and three days growth of beard roughened his face. Bright blue eyes deeply set inspected his messenger Selah.

"Come up higher and enjoy my hospitality!" Rivoas spoke to all of them.

They walked the last 20 paces up the final switchback trail which led to the cave opening where Selah had always seen Rivoas. That perch over looked, from near to far, the forest, then the city, then the fertile 20 stanion strip between the city and the Great Ocean. The cave opening stretched into the mountain to the north, a channel through the rock wide enough for ten men to walk side by side with a ceiling of eight paces or more. But it was dark and none could see more than 40 paces into it.

"I believe you know each other," Rivoas spoke to Keeres and Selah as they approached the fire where Skud sat.

"We do," Skud replied for them in a bland tone sitting cross legged by the fire staring blankly into it.

Selah's bliss was interrupted at the sight of him and she was inwardly jealous that she should be sharing Rivoas and her adventure with the likes of Skud.

"Very well, brothers and sisters all! Please join me for breakfast," Rivoas added with a welcoming tone.

However, before anyone could join Skud by the fire, Keeres and Selah caught the panoramic view from the cave opening. Keeres was now seeing as clearly as Selah, and what a first sight it was that greeted his eyes. He stood at the mouth of the cave with his arms hanging limp at his side and his mouth agape. Selah, though accustomed to her new vision by now, also stood amazed.

"Papa, can you see? Can you see?"

By the tears welling up in his eyes, Selah gathered that he could.

"Papa, look at the big tree and the hole we came in and the city from wall to wall and the Great Ocean and the ships! Oh it is beautiful!" Selah gushed, forgetting about Skud behind her.

"Selah, I can see our house; look over there just past the stadium!" Keeres pointed her to the spot.

"Oh, yes, and there are the stables and the square and the booths and everything!" Selah was utterly delighted. Delighted enough even to speak to Skud, "Skud, can you see it all?"

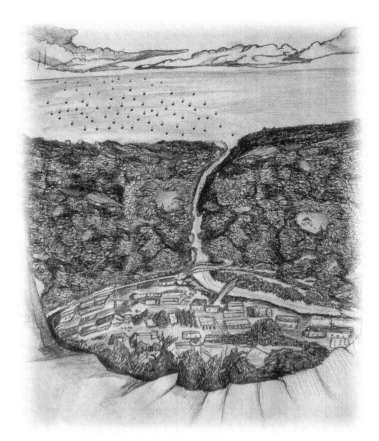

Keeres' view from the cave opening

Surprisingly, Skud answered without an attack, "Yes I can, Selah,"

He had not called her by that name since she was a baby, and Selah took note.

"Skud, you can see! Skud, maybe we can be friends now!" Selah was emboldened by Skud's softening.

"Skud is thinking over many things just now Selah. It may be better to leave that for another day," Rivoas redirected.

"Skud fell down like a dead man when we first got here, heehaaaa!" Kwea slapped his knee with delight, for the first time having one up on Skud.

Skud started to lunge over at Kwea but Rivoas was between them and the attempt wilted into a seething scowl pointed in Kwea's direction.

"We got here in the dark and couldn't see much no how but when we woked up and seen this here sight it was like we came alive for the first time!" Kwea happily finished his story as he chewed on a bit of the roasted rabbit from the fire of Rivoas.

This minor episode between Kwea and Skud gave Keeres just enough time to gather his thoughts and he assembled enough courage to directly question Rivoas, "Sir, who are you, where are you from, and what is the meaning of all this talk of escaping north?"

Keeres was finding it hard to keep a single train of thought. He was also beginning to feel small and dirty as he gazed at the face of Rivoas.

"All in due time, brother Keeres. You have been a faithful watcher for many years and a seeker of the way. It is why you were chosen to find the child," Rivoas replied.

"What way? How do you know me? What manner of man are you that can bestow miraculous vision at will? Such powers are not natural."

Keeres was amazed by this man but had spent decades building walls of caution and skepticism regarding the dealings of men, so was slow to offer complete trust. He knew that the legends also contained tales of beautiful demons.

"What is 'natural', Keeres?" Rivoas turned the questioning around. "Your learned men relegate such wonders as you have now experienced to the realm of the supernatural, but only because they believe *their* world to be the only true natural order. It is with this assumption that the mistake is made. Maraldia is not presently in a natural state of existence. In fact, it would be more accurate to say it languishes in the realm of the 'subnatural'. Come with me Keeres, and I will take you to the land of the truly natural."

Keeres puzzled over the words of Rivoas.

Rivoas continued, "Do you see the vast array of ships, Keeres?"

Keeres let his eyes and mind settle on the enormous armada surrounding the ocean side of Maraldia. It only took half a second for him to realize that this armada was ten times too many to be Maraldian. He remembered the words of Rohon and the ship's figurehead carved in the image of a sorcerer.

"Are you from the ships?" Keeres questioned.

"Those on the ships would claim that we are all one race and they would speak truly. But there is more to brotherhood than flesh and bone. The ships are from the people who call themselves Freemen, for they have forever freed themselves from that which they despise," Rivoas' words were riddles to Keeres.

"What do they despise, and why are they here?" Keeres sought practical information.

"They come to free you after their own manner. Those who wish it will follow them. Those who do not will come to me. Those who refuse to decide have decided," Rivoas spoke in grave tones.

"Come to you where? To go where?" Keeres questioned, emotion evident in his words. He felt he knew but had to hear it. He paced and motioned with his arms while all eyes fixed on the exchange between he and Rivoas, "To the sunlit throne of the cave map? What is that place and how should we go?"

"You have always known of it. When you are still you know it best," Rivoas looked directly into the eyes of Keeres with a faint smile as he spoke.

Keeres felt a surge of something like joy in his chest and had the impulse to laugh out loud but successfully kept it repressed, though it almost took his breath away.

"You must tell as many as you can, and you will have help. They will hear and know as well," Rivoas finished with more riddles.

"Papa, look at the square! There is a big crowd of people and they are banging on the door to the police station! Will Noble be alright? Are they coming to get Noble?! Poor Noble!" Selah fretted.

"When darkness falls on the final festival day there will be nothing left to decide. All that was hidden will be exposed. Be swift, the time has come," Rivoas finished these last words as he pulled the cloak over his head and sat down to slowly stir the fire.

"Then what? People are going to want to know why and what happens next!" Keeres questioned. He was imagining how foolish he may look trying to relay such a message. Rivoas did not look up but slowly stirred the fire.

"Is there anything more?" Keeres insisted.

Rivoas silently stirred the fire and Keeres had that same shameful feeling as yesterday when he flashed a sarcastic smile up to the unseen mountain.

"Papa, let's go try to tell people and see what happens next. And oh, let's go to the police station right away, I'm afraid for Noble," Selah spoke as she pointed out over the city.

At this Keeres strapped on his pack, lit his lamps and headed into the tunnel, Skud and Kwea close behind.

Back at the police station Noble looked out through a small barred window near the ceiling at the angry mob beginning to set fire to the station.

As Keeres and Selah were groping in the dark that third festival day for the hidden key to Noble's shop, the High council members were already at the ocean's edge boarding a lifeboat heading toward the lead Freemen vessel.

"Honored Donem, please give us a fair summary of the fleet we are about to observe," Lered spoke, eager to understand his position better.

"Please Council Chair, address me as Donem as you would a brother," Donem replied, beginning their voyage with a gesture of peace after yesterday's challenge.

"Certainly, and Lered I shall be to you."

Lered conceded this courtesy though left his guard fully intact.

Donem continued as the lifeboat pulled away from shore, "Our fleet of 813 is made up of various ships. The largest are nearly 130 paces in length and can carry almost 1,000 passengers. The smallest and fastest are a mere 30 paces and carry 50 comfortably, by seagoing standards. The mix overall can transport more than 600,000 souls, a floating city for sure," Donem said with a certain technological pride.

"That is enough for all, our latest census of the city and furthest settlements puts our population at roughly 550,000. You have estimated well," Lered calculated.

"You can see that with such a fleet my sense of care is extreme. Never in the history of this ocean have so many vessels been afloat at the same time. Our losses would be staggering if we lingered into the winds of winter. Suppose the tempest should arrive even a day early? The risk is already great. The entire enterprise is staggering as you can now see, almost a fool's gamble."

Donem guffawed a bit playing the part of the Great Captain concerned for his loyal crew and wishing to impress the great generosity of the entire Freemen venture upon Lered.

"I do see, Donem," Lered's words emphasized their newly established informality, "Please tell me of the logistics. Surely you have thought through the loading and resupply of ships. How shall all this be accomplished in the remaining days before the winds?"

These analytical considerations temporarily took Lered's mind off of the larger shocking enterprise foist upon him.

"Yes, of course. I am glad to hear you speak of the practical matters for they are considerable. We have had to adjust our original plans, as I said, since the travel here delayed us by weeks leaving precious little time for pleasantries. My best men have calculated that we can board and resupply the ships in four days if given good weather, but we will need to work around the clock. We have planned to stage 30 ships along the shore at a time and we will give each vessel an average of three hours to board and resupply before moving out to sea. But we will need your people to be ready at the shore. My men will work with yours to stage the boarding from the beach. Each citizen shall bring half the stores required for a four month journey to supplement our existing reserves. Only minimal personal belongings shall be allowed, as much as an individual can carry after supplying the required provisions. We shall supply the water and wish permission to access your great river as soon as possible," Donem spoke quickly, clicking down his checklist.

Lered only paid minimal attention as he rolled through his mind the planned town meetings later that day. His thoughts tumbled forward:

~ 107 ~

It is a tall order to announce to the people in the evening that there are aliens in boats on their shore waiting to take them away from everything they have ever known, and then instruct them that they should be ready to leave by morning! It is almost laughable! The people will need more than four days just to overcome the psychological shock of finding that they are no longer the only people in the world. Then there is the planning and logistics. Such an effort should be given weeks if not months to plan. I cannot imagine anything but pure chaos by trying to execute such an exodus in four days.

He interrupted his mental meanderings to answer Donem, "You may access the Elif at daybreak tomorrow but if I am any judge of Maraldian sensibilities I can tell you that fully two thirds of the population will not be willing to decide such a matter under pressure. I'm afraid that though your generosity and personal risk have been great, many of your ships will return empty."

"That is for each man to decide. It does not diminish my mission," Donem showed that it did diminish his mission by his very manner of speaking. "However," Donem quickly adopted a more calculated tone, "I would appreciate a fair hearing at your public meetings this evening. Given that fear of the unknown may rob many of this great opportunity, I believe words of encouragement from a wise council chair could strike a reasonable counterbalance."

Lered let those comments rest on the turbulent waters through which they plowed. Lered now for the first time caught a glimpse of Donem's lead vessel. As they approached the bow of the ship the figurehead loomed large in view. Lered believed he had seen it before but could not put his finger on where. Keeres would have been able to tell him.

"This way, gentlemen," said Donem, directing as they moored to a floating loading platform.

Upon the platform were wide stairs leading to an opening in the hull five paces over their head. The council members were

~ 108 ~

truly astonished as they took in the sheer mass of the Freemen's largest ship. No Maraldian ship would think of designing an access door into the side of such a vessel. The technology of the Freemen again astounded the council.

"She is seaworthy, eh?" Ceresin thought aloud to Donem as he piled out of the lifeboat, "With a hole in her and all?"

"She seals well, my dear Ceresin. In fact there are six such openings in this vessel," Donem replied with a superior grin. "We have been sailing such ships for more than 100 years."

Once on the platform the council members were greeted by the ship's captain and led up the stairs into the ship's hold.

"Half of these stores would sink the stoutest Maraldian ship!" Councilmen Sapsion whispered to Lered as they investigated, wide-eyed.

The hold was a vast maze of large chambers connected by wide hallways. Presently they mounted another stair and found themselves in an array of sleeping chambers, mostly large rooms of stacked bunks.

"Families will need to endure the loss of privacy during the voyage as you can see, but this was an essential compromise in the ship's construction to ensure maximum passenger capacity," the captain explained.

Three enormous kitchens were found one deck above with large open eating areas adjoined, each with row upon row of benches and tables built into the decking.

"Other than the sleeping quarters, this is likely to be the place where most of the voyage is passed. A social hall of sorts," the captain explained, proudly showing off the accommodations.

Unopened crates of cooking and eating utensils were stacked against the walls and secured with ropes, awaiting the

Maraldians. There were numerous smaller rooms on this deck along the outer perimeter of the eating area with windows to the sea.

"You will notice that we have left a large open area to one end which can be used for games or dancing to pass the time," Donem interjected. The Freemen had thought of everything.

"The main deck will be off limits to all but sailors, of which the qualified Maraldians will be included. Riggings and all manner of sailing apparatus are no place for the novice sea voyager," the captain said as he concluded the tour of the first ship.

Several smaller vessels were also inspected in like manner before the morning was over, all equally impressive.

"Donem, tell me of your proposed arrangements back in Freeland for such a mass immigration. What lands and jobs shall our people occupy given that we bring nothing with us? Suppose every man, woman and child were to make the journey? Can Freeland possibly manage the economic impact?" Lered queried as he pieced together the entire picture for the afternoon's announcements.

"The impact is not insignificant but surely much smaller than you imagine. Absorbing your entire population would represent to us less than half of one percent increase in total population. We are more than 300 million souls in Freeland," Donem commented casually while stepping back into the lifeboat. "And we have thousands of miles of unexplored lands for those wishing to pioneer, and plenty of room for tradesmen in the cities. Housing has been promised to each family in one or the other and temporary settlements are already in place."

Lered was reeling at the thought of a nation 500 times the size of Maraldia. So many people. How could it be governed? What resources are needed to support such a population? He was feeling very small and stared vacantly at Donem.

"I can see that this surprises you, Lered," Donem chuckled, "but do not be alarmed by the size of things. Day to day life shall not be quite so different, only the opportunities far more bountiful." Donem seemed to promise a paradise.

As they finished boarding the lifeboat for the return to land, Lered calculated his evening speech. He would be needing it sooner than he thought.

Lered had sworn everyone associated with yesterday's interview of Donem to absolute secrecy until the formal citywide meetings could be held the next day. All were in agreement and swore a solemn oath. What he had not counted on was the unsworn police officers, who had heard Donem's impellor blast, essentially torturing the truth out of the poor page boy. The police officers had taken their juicy news and spread it all around the Winter Winds that night.

By the time Lered was stepping out onto the sand and preparing for the hour long ride back to the city, a crowd was already gathering in the city square.

"We'll get the truth outta them or there will be nothing left of these fine looking Capitol buildings before long!" threatened one irate citizen who had heard the rumors at the tavern last night. "Bring out Lered!" he demanded to the officer on duty at the steps of the Capitol.

The crowd of 100, and growing fast, supported him.

"All council members are absent at present," the officer stated three steps above the crowd and keeping one hand on his sword.

"Absent are they?" challenged another man. "I saw Councilman Torund go up these steps not five minutes ago!"

In fact, Councilman Torund did not go that morning to the ships. He was serving in a temporary capacity with the council in place of his ailing father and only for a few more days until the scheduled ballot shortly after the festival. He was short and bald and very round. He actually had little interest in council matters but was forced to represent his father under Maraldian tradition. He had been in council yesterday and heard the entire interview but, feeling that the temporary nature of his assignment afforded him minimal accountability, considered it better to attend to personal matters that morning.

"Bring us Torund!" shouted the first man.

"Bring us Torund!" shouted the second.

"Bring us Torund! Bring us Torund! Bring us Torund!" chanted the crowd in unison.

Torund was just inside behind the great wooden doors listening to the entire affair. Oh how he now wished he had gone with the rest to the ships. He glanced across the room to the sergeant at the desk who looked at the rotund little man with a measure of disgust, cowering behind the door.

"*Some* leader," mumbled the sergeant under his breath.

The sentry on the steps was doing the best he could to calm the situation but some in the crowd began to pile scrap wood against the building and threatened with torches to burn the place down if they did not get information immediately. Inside Noble stood upon his stool to look out the narrow window high on his cell wall. He called for Torund as well.

The sentry motioned for silence and opened the door a crack, "Councilman Torund I believe your duty calls. Tell them what you know or make something up if you don't."

"I can't do it," Torund whimpered.

"*Do it* or you will become intimate with the point of my blade," threatened the desk sergeant, who now stood to enable a clear view of the stiletto on his belt.

"I am a member of the high council and you threaten me?" Torund was indignant at being threatened and it piqued within him a measure of defiance.

"By the time they dig us all out of the charred remains of this building your term will be expired," the Sergeant rejoined as he went for his blade.

Torund swallowed hard and looked at the floor, his hand reaching for the edge of the door. He took a step outside.

"RAAAHAAA!" The crowd roared now feeling their collective power at the sight of their demands yielding results.

"Councilman Torund, tell us all you know of these rumors. Is Maraldia being invaded by wizards from across the Great Ocean? Shall we all be forced like slaves aboard their ships? Come now, speak plainly. Where is the rest of the council?" questioned the lead citizen.

Murmurings and shuffling were quieted by Torund's trembling raised hand, "I am not at liberty to discuss these matters, you should wait for the appointed meetings…"

"RAAAAHAAAA!!!!!" the crowd erupted into such a roar that Noble fell off his stool from within his cell.

All manner of arm thrusting and chest beating were now apparent among the angry mob as they edged closer to the steps brandishing lit torches.

The sentry leaned over to Torund, "For the Givers sake man, make something up!"

Torund was visibly shaking now and again slowly raised his hand to quiet the crowd. He was not clever enough to weave a convincing impromptu lie so he spoke what he knew hoping to reveal as little as possible and escape.

"My dear countrymen," he began.

Grumblings and impatient mutterings met his words, "Save it for the council Torund! Give it to us short and straight!" demanded the second lead citizen.

"Yes! Yes!" was heard throughout the crowd.

"Alright, of course. Yesterday the high council of Maraldia was visited by a man claiming to be from a vast nation across the Great Ocean. He is not a wizard though he has brought to us advanced inventions from that place as gifts," Torund explained.

"Weapons he brought! Machines for killing!" interrupted a thin man shouting from the middle of the crowd.

"YAAAAHAAA!!!" the crowd echoed the thin man's apprehensions.

"QUIET!!!" shouted the sentry, and the crowd quieted.

"If these visitors are bent on conquest they could have done it easily enough given their great numbers," Torund echoed Lered's thoughts from the day before.

"How great?" questioned the first citizen.

"It is said that there are hundreds of ships. The council has gone to verify just this morning," Torund explained.

The crowd murmured again and before Torund could explain the offer to immigrate to Freeland the remaining council members and Donem returned via carriage to the Capitol. The agitated crowd recognized the council members and pressed in upon the carriages. Torund took it as his chance to escape. The crowd and carriages became one jumbled mass of motion and noise as everyone pressed in to see Lered and this wizard from across the ocean. Lered attempted to step from the carriage, but frightened and fearful hands clutched and tore at him forcing him to retreat into the carriage for a semblance of safety.

Keeres and Selah arrived in the square at noon as the tumult reached a fever pitch, the irrational crowd jostling the carriages to and fro; arrived just in time to hear three shots from the impellor of Donem pierce the noisy riot.

13

The shots had their desired effect. The crowd moved away from the carriage just long enough for Lered to slide out and quickly mount the steps of the Capitol building. He was glad to have spent the ride back from the shore thinking about how to address the citizens and now he smoothed his tussled hair and motioned with his hand for silence.

"People of Maraldia, have I been naïve all these years to have thought better of you than what I now see in this raucous assembly?" Lered's words stung them like a father come home early to find his children engaged in a drinking party. Rohon was in the crowd and felt it most.

"Council Chair Lered, please forgive us this foolishness but explain the frightful reports we've heard," Rohon spoke the mind of all. He had been at the Winter Winds the night before hoping to find Keeres but instead finding the babbling policemen.

"As to what you have heard I cannot say, but I will tell you all I know if you will stand peaceably," Lered spoke as he gave Donem an instructive glance to stay hidden in the carriage.

Keeres recognized Rohon and looked for a safe place to deposit Selah so he could get to the front of the crowd with his old friend and hear what Lered was saying. He found a sturdy festival booth and perched Selah on top of it, giving her a perfect view of the entire proceeding. Keeres sidled up to Rohon with a smile.

"It appears that you are not crazy after all old friend," Keeres whispered. He assumed this commotion had something to do with the armada he had seen from the mountain.

Lered's skills as an orator and diplomat were on full display as the crowd grew to over a thousand. He confidently stood on the steps of the Capitol building announcing to the amazed throng that their tightly circumscribed world had just been expanded to almost unimaginable breadth; it was his finest hour as patriarch of Maraldia.

As Lered spoke, Selah surveyed the situations in both the square and the mountain cave from her booth-top perch on the back edge of the square across from the Capitol steps. As she gazed at the bulging square and then to the figure of Rivoas on the mountain she began to feel a strange trembling inside her chest. She watched as Rivoas stood and raised his hands to the sky and something inside compelled her to rise as well. The trembling was uncomfortable and for a moment she thought she would be sick and doubled over grasping her stomach.

"Hhhgggmm," she groaned softly while keeping an eye on both the near and far spectacles, and the groaning soothed her.

"Hummmm," she closed her eyes and continued the soft groaning until it became a pure hum.

Selah felt as if she were in a dream and straightened up fully as the humming completely cleared the discomfort in her chest. Eyes still closed, she followed the impulse to open her mouth as the humming progressed into a pure single note song. As Selah raised her hands to the sky the song increased in volume and began to gain the attention of those standing nearest to the booth. Her song now moved rhythmically from one pure tone to the next and seemed to gain a volume impossible for a lone singer. Soon the entire square, including Lered, had stopped to fix their attention solely on this other worldly sound, afraid to breathe lest they pollute the heavenly song.

Selah's song

In the carriage Donem covered his ears in writhing agony.

The stillness of the crowd and the angelic song lasted only a moment longer until Selah became aware that more than 1,000 sets of eyes were fixed upon her.

The song trailed off and Selah, as though it were the grand finale of her private symphony spoke, "Please, all of you must follow me to the mountain and escape to the north! Rivoas will lead us, there will be nothing left of Maraldia by the end of the festival! Please, everyone must escape through the cave in the forest by the big old tree near the mountain!"

At these words the crowd was shaken from their trance and one of them shouted, "It's the crazy little girl who disrupted the festival yesterday!"

A few people began to laugh and then most began to laugh until you would have thought that Lered's astounding news had been completely forgotten.

"Listen, please listen!" Selah shouted to no avail.

Just then, though no one had noticed the sudden assault of thick storm clouds rolling in from the Great Ocean, a torrential rain began as though someone had thrown a bucket of water on a fire. The laughing, grumbling, and soaked crowd now scurried in every direction to look for cover.

"No! Wait! Please listen!" Selah pleaded. Then looking up to the mountain and throwing her hands down in frustration, "They won't listen! They are running away!"

Selah implored and wept until the entire square had emptied. The rain came down in torrents as she looked to the mountain and collapsed to her knees atop the booth, face in her hands. Keeres just stood staring up at the child he had picked from among the wolves, while Rivoas smiled down on them both.

14

As soon as the rain subsided, heralds were sent into every corner of the city and to the farthest reaches of the eastern and western settlements, message from Lered in hand. Couriers with swift horses relayed the message up and down the length of the protective Tolis handing off to a fresh steed and rider every 20 stanion, enabling the entire city-state to receive important news within a day and a half. Donem had arranged for ships to sail east and west to rendezvous with those in outlying settlements so that all would not have to travel to Maraldia proper to board his ships.

Lered had dictated the message to 40 scribes who quickly multiplied copies, rolled, and sealed them; enough for every needed venue within Maraldia. As he finished the instructions related to the Freemen's offer he paused, and every scribe's eye was upon him waiting for the traditional formal ending of all such proclamations.

However, instead of the usual final salutation, Lered continued his message, "In addition, it is worth noting that the astounding revelation described above is not the only miraculous message in the streets of Maraldia during this time of festival. A young girl, born under astonishing circumstances," for Lered had remembered Selah from the day of Keeres impassioned plea, "has brought us a message to flee the city through an unknown northern passage. The veracity of her claims I cannot substantiate in rational terms. However, a very unusual and striking song she has brought to us this very day, unlike any ever heard, and it persuades me to include this addendum. Indeed a song that would make you believe you had never heard a true sound in your life by comparison. She speaks of a northern passage in the face of the Tolis near an ancient tree. It would appear to be madness, but I would be remiss not to inform you fully of all late proceedings. May the Givers carry you forth. Council Chair of Maraldia, I am Lered."

Donem stood nearby and objected immediately, "Council Chair, in this time of difficult decisions for your people it is irresponsible to muddle their thinking with the foolish ramblings of an insane child. I strongly object and request that the addendum be stricken from the proclamation. This can lead to no good end."

Every scribe sat with pen in hand and stared intently at the two men standing a few handbreadths apart locked in each other's gaze.

Lered broke the silence, "I am quite surprised to hear the representative of a nation calling itself 'Free' land express opposition to each citizen's free choice based on all available information. Without all true accounts set forth can you really call it 'choice?' Can you really call it 'free?' It becomes little better than manipulation. What I have written I have written. Send the couriers," Lered kept his gaze fixed on Donem as he spoke.

Donem turned in his usual way of swirling coat tails, exiting the chamber.

As one man every scribe immediately put pen to parchment and scurried to produce the required copies. Before midafternoon the first settlements were receiving the message.

That evening in the home of Keeres his small family huddled near the fireplace. The nights were growing colder and the winter would soon be upon them. Discussion of the afternoon's events had not yet been discussed. It was all too strange.

Finally Locenes spoke, "Selah, tell me of this song. What is this thing that has been announced far and wide? I only wish I would have been there."

Selah was embarrassed and blushed, "I don't know. It just came out. It had to come out or I would have died trying to keep it in!"

Just then there was a knock at the door. Keeres opened it to the face of Rohon, and not only he but a multitude with him, some familiar and some not. Keeres stood staring.

"Well that's a fine welcome from my old friend, a gawking face that would scare a ghost. Will you invite us in or should we be on our way?" Rohon cajoled in usual manner.

"No, no… please come in. It's a bit small for such a crowd but you are all welcome if you don't mind standing," Keeres replied as he regained himself.

The crowd piled in, a fair cross section of Maraldia. Tall, short, fat, thin, ragged and rich alike. They seemed in a pleasant mood considering all the consternation about the city at the moment.

"I stood you up at the Winter Winds, and I see you've brought the party to me old Rohon. But I'm afraid I haven't enough ale in the place for such a crowd. What can I offer you instead?"

Keeres was beginning to catch the mood of the moment while Locenes and Selah looked on from the hearth.

"Well, good Keeres, you can explain to us why you've kept such secrets from your best and oldest friends all these years. Each of us was in the square today when the news of these Freemen broke and each of us heard your sweet daughter sing the purest song we ever heard. Then to top all of that she goes on about escaping the city. That's a lot for a common man to swallow in a lifetime much less an hour. But something about that girl of yours…that's why we're here," Rohon finished amidst nodding heads and quiet statements of concurrence.

"But you all laughed at me!" Selah couldn't help gushing forth the hurt she felt.

Rohon came forward and bent down on one knee to be eye to eye with Selah. "Most did, sweet Selah, and I'm sorry for that, but not a soul in this room took your message for anything but the words of the Givers themselves. That's why we're here. We need to know what to do next."

Selah looked at her father with a smile and jumped off the hearth into the arms of Rohon, "There is a man with a bright face, Daddy has seen him too. His name is Rivoas. I can see him from here, I can see all the way to the mountain! Anyone who goes to the mountain can see as good as me, even Skud!" Selah could not get the story out fast enough.

The evening progressed with Keeres relaying the entire story to the group, from the finding of Selah at the wall, to the trip up the mountain and even to the sorcerer of the festival ornaments that Rohon saw on the Freemen ships.

"Here, please pass these," said Locenes as she found something in her stores to refresh everyone.

"Selah, something burned within me as I stood in the square today and listened to your song. I cannot explain it, but it spoke truer to me than any wise man's words," an old woman spoke with passion.

Many testified similarly and not a few wept aloud. Some testified that there was something in all of the day's events that resonated with the old stories that most had assigned to the station of fable. Others worried that the Freemen were not to be trusted but could not explain how they came to such a conclusion.

They ended their evening by vowing to spread the message for the remainder of the festival days to any that would hear. Any that had doubts could investigate by visiting the ancient tree and the cave into the mountain. None knew exactly how events would unfold in the next few days but each left determined that if they had to flee, it would be through the mountain and not across the ocean.

15

Even before the sun rose on the fourth day of the festival, Maraldians from city and settlements alike began arriving on the shore ready to board the ships. Most first-takers were those hungry for fulfillment of Donem's promise, a life of plenty and ease. These journeyed through the night carrying all they could in spite of instructions to travel light. The end result, after only a few ferry runs, was a beach littered with innumerable personal belongings forcibly left behind. Grandmother's favorite painting and daughter's favorite doll rolled together in the foamy surf.

Amid this mild form of predawn chaos, Skud was meeting with his gang up an alleyway, not having yet retired for the night. His newfound vision provided him a distinct advantage in his usual business, but his appetite for such escapades had diminished since the meeting with Rivoas. There was no hiding the entire affair in the mountain from the gang no matter how much Skud threatened Kwea. Kwea was just too delighted with his vision and the entire tumult of the city to give thought to how anything he might say would be interpreted. The gang had a good laugh on Skud as Kwea relayed the fainting episode but knew better than to take it too far. Skud could still best them all if it came to fisticuffs.

"Let's get out of here right now," Jojus implored, "either north or south seems better than what's goin' on here."

"Do you have any idea how much stuff is gonna be left fer us after half this city moves out? Every other house on the street is gonna be up for grabs. In a couple days we'll all be rich!" Skud countered, but without convincing enthusiasm.

"Didn't the crazy girl say that nothing would be left of the city after the festival? What about that? What was that supposed to mean?" Jojus queried.

"Nobody know what she mean. SHE don't even know what she mean. She's only seven stinkin' years old," Skud's internal irritation was coming to the surface as he spoke.

"But what about the bright faced guy, Skud, what about all his words? You seen him and he were real. Roversa ur sumthin' like that," Kwea was excited to have some firsthand knowledge to work with for a change and spoke more than normal.

"Rivoas, his name is Rivoas. I know what he said. You shut up now. He talked in riddles and you don't even understand plain talk...Mister Halfshirt," Skud scolded and insulted but not so much as in the past. "Let's wait and see. We got a couple days to check things out."

The gang got a chuckle out of Kwea's funny looking shirt, and it was enough to silence him for now. The gang agreed to wait it out, but in the meantime helped themselves to any vacant house they spotted.

As the sun finally dawned, Rohon and Keeres rode through the city looking for opportunities to spread their invitation.

"The festival is no more, Keeres," Rohon's expression was serious.

Booths in the square were in various stages of disassembly when normally they would have been enjoying peak business.

"Yes, instead of dancers and musicians filling the streets, everywhere people talk in small groups and the occasional family trundles toward the ocean," Keeres likewise spoke in contemplative tones.

Little business was being conducted except as it related to daily living needs.

"These Freemen heralds smell to me of death, Keeres. Up and down every street shouting instructions and reassurances.

Promises of fortune and ease and opportunity bouncing off every brick building and into the open windows of the citizenry," Rohon's horse clopped along slowly, punctuating his words.

"I saw Darrsce with them, promising double portions of property to those who would leave today, along with tepid warnings about being left behind," Keeres glanced at Rohon as he spoke, and Rohon returned a raised eyebrow.

"He is skilled in persuasion, and adds legitimacy to the message as a Maraldian and a council member. I wonder if the land promises are true."

In fact, Keeres suspicions were correct; Darrsce's promises were not assured by the Freemen.

Freemen move through the streets

"Our small group from last night will be busy today spreading the message of a northern passage. They have already begun. On the way to your house some in the streets stopped to ask me if it were true that something much better than either Freeland or Maraldia lay due north," Rohon commented with a smile.

"And what did you tell them?" Keeres returned.

"I told them yes, and that it would be better not to wait too long to decide about going," Rohon continued. "In fact, they told me that people by the dozens were already heading for the forest. Even people in outlying settlements upon hearing the proclamation of Lered were heading toward the city with only enough provisions for the one way journey."

"Imagine that. These people have heard only one part in a hundred of this strange story, yet they leave everything and come. I'm sure they are considered madmen by most. I am in the midst and hardly know what to make of it. I have seen the mountain and been given new sight and still feel as though I don't understand," Keeres poured out his doubts to Rohon as they clopped past the square.

"Yes, madmen. Perhaps we are madmen too, Keeres. The vast majority do nothing at all. I speak to them and they are content to wait it out. My wife as well. Life for her is good enough and neither promises of enormous wealth nor threats of impending doom move her from what she is comfortable with. She believes it will all pass in a few weeks and Maraldia will continue on as always. Better not to be too rash," Rohon also questioned himself with these musings.

After a morning's ride through the city speaking to all who would hear, Keeres and Rohon headed to the ships for a firsthand look at the Freemen armada, and for old time's sake.

"Those were good days, you and I on the boats," Keeres reminisced as they hitched their horses and headed to Rohon's personal skiff.

"Not good enough to keep you there," Rohon jabbed.

He had missed Keeres when he left fishing to tend stables.

Except for a grin, Keeres ignored the comment saying, "Let's follow that ship out to deeper water, the one that is just finishing loading and weighing anchor."

And so they did, unnoticed by the Freemen sailors in all the commotion.

"Look at the size of it. Rohon, your estimates were far too small," Keeres gushed as they rowed alongside.

"Well, please remember that your friends are not so fortunate as to have the vision of a mountain hawk," Rohon reminded Keeres of what he had already come to take for granted.

"Yes, sorry," was his only reply.

Keeres seemed to be preoccupied with the deck sailors on the ship they were tracking.

"What is it?" Rohon sensed the distraction but could not see what Keeres was seeing.

"They appear to be having a disagreement, a Maraldian sailor and a Freemen sailor. I cannot hear what they are saying. The other Freemen sailors are joining the fray. Oh, isn't that good sport? Four Freemen sailors against one Maraldian, shoving and jeering. Yes lovely, now three of them have pushed his back against the mast and tied his hands around the back of it, laughing and punching. So this is what the Freemen have in store for us? What? WHAT?" Keeres stood up in the skiff.

"What is it Keeres?! Speak it!" Rohon's heart was pounding.

Keeres could not speak it and stood open mouthed. The fourth Freemen sailor had found a harpoon on deck and pinned the

Maraldian sailor to the mast through the chest, to the howls and laughter of his Freemen comrades.

What would have been day five of the joyous festival began in gloom as a drizzly rain shrouded the city. No players or hawkers filled the streets, only abandoned banners, stages and booths accompanied by an increased number of Freemen heralds.

"Help for anyone going to the shore! Wagons for your goods and carriages for the old! Come be reunited with the ancient brotherhood! Now is the day of your greatest fortune! The Freemen await you with open arms! Don't spend the rest of your life regretting your decision to stay!" announced the Freemen heralds.

The message had begun to take a slightly more negative tone and by the end of the day the message bordered on dire.

"The ships have begun to leave! Your countrymen have made the good choice for Freeland and you may never see them again! Don't spend the rest of your lives in this island prison! Come while there is still time!" the evening heralds cajoled.

Most Maraldians bided their time waiting to see what the others would do. By the end of that dreary day only about one fourth of the population had made for the beaches. A much smaller fraction, though not insignificant, had made their way to the Tolis. Rumors swirled regarding those who went to the mountain. Scoffers wondered what had become of them. Had they been killed by a beast of the forest? Were they hiding, waiting for someone to show the promised way? None of the doubting minds ever considered the possibility that they had actually found what they were looking for. Yet their absence fueled more interest and many began to explore, if only for curiosity's sake. They had come back confirming the existence of an underground tunnel at the base of an enormous tree, though few of the merely curious dared follow any further. But even such broadened testimony, and that from respected citizens (unlike the rantings of a little girl), were mostly brushed aside.

Meanwhile Keeres took time to petition the courts for the release of Noble. Unfortunately those with authority to release a prisoner were not so easily found in the current commotion. After hours of waiting at the jail and procedural paperwork, Keeres was out of options and stopped to see his old friend on the way out.

"Keeres! I had concluded that I would be the only Maraldian left by week's end, all others having sailed on. You wouldn't happen to have the key to this door now would you old friend?" Noble was profoundly glad to see his friend and it bubbled out in lighthearted banter.

"I have spent the better part of the day trying to acquire that very item but to no avail. Tell me, how much do you know about the affairs of the city these last few days?" Keeres spoke as he pulled up a bench.

"I know whatever I could get from that high window there. I saw the commotion two days ago and feared I would be roasted alive in this cell watching men with torches gather. I know that men from across the ocean have arrived with great promises for any who will leave with them in a hurry; that much is everywhere in the streets. And just before the storm I heard a sound coming from the front of the building I think, from the square. Some instrument of heaven, a pure tone. I cannot describe it. I don't think I breathed for a full minute as I listened," Noble recounted as best he could.

"It was Selah," Keeres said plainly.

"What? What do you mean?" Noble was stunned.

"I can't explain it. She can't explain it. Something inside her needed to come out. She pleaded with the crowd from the top of the booth to escape to the north. Then the storm," Keeres continued, relaying everything he and Selah had discovered, all about Rivoas and the tunnel in the mountain leading to who knows where.

"And what shall *you* do?" Noble finally queried, making the emphasis personal.

The question caught Keeres by surprise. Up until now the events of each day had kept him occupied. He had not fully rationalized what he would himself do as the final day of the festival approached. Rivoas had said that nothing would remain of Maraldia by the end of the festival. Did he believe it? Was he willing to bet the future of his family upon it; to actually leave everything behind? The whole situation was crazy. He had always prided himself on leaving room for the mystical in his thinking but now that the thing was upon him he questioned all the more. He remembered the words of Rivoas, "Those who refuse to decide, have decided."

"What are you waiting for, Keeres?"

Noble read the silence of Keeres accurately and gave him a look as though to say, *you old fool, this is what you were born for.*

It was all that Keeres needed to bring clarity.

"Why only for you, Noble. If you had not gotten yourself into trouble we would all be gone by now," Keeres quickly barbed back.

The decision had brought sudden peace to Keeres. Whatever lay through that mountain tunnel, it would be his future and the future of his family.

"Don't go anywhere, I'll be back tomorrow with keys," Keeres joked as he got up to leave.

Noble just grinned as he watched his friend depart.

On what would have been the morning of the sixth day of the festival, the mood in the city was somber. So many families had been torn apart, some members choosing to stay and others choosing to go. Some headed for the forest never to be seen again, to the utter dismay of their loved ones who thought them mad.

And the message of the Freemen had turned to complete insult.

"This is the last chance for all of you fools who have waited until the final hour! Do you think we will wait while the coming tempest blows apart our ships? Come now or regret it forever!" The few remaining heralds shouted.

But not everyone was in dismay. Stohl had no intention of going anywhere and, though he had not done a trace of work in years, took this occasion to loot any vacant house he could find. His paradise had finally come.

"Boy, I think it's time you an' me parted ways," Stohl taunted his son, "I'm tired a' providin' fer you while you waste yer days knocking around the streets with yer no good friends."

In reality, Stohl realized he no longer needed Skud's income and had no intention of sharing his own newfound wealth.

"Sure thing, Pops," was all Skud would say.

Stohl was a little disappointed with the lack of effect his rejection seemed to have on Skud but was in a generous mood so did not retort with the usual back of his hand.

As the day wore into midafternoon, all sounds of the heralds had been silenced. Apparently the morning's insults had truly been the last call. In fact, the entire city was eerily quiet. Rohon, along with several others, made their way to the house of Keeres to plan for the next day. Similar small meetings were happening throughout the city and many north seekers from the outlying settlements were now arriving and receiving a fuller account of the week's events. As darkness took over that sixth day, Keeres related to the small group at his house what he had seen on the Freemen ship the day before. They all shuddered at the images he painted and were all the more convinced to make the trek north tomorrow. They had spread the message as far as they could in the available time and now it was time to go.

As the visitors moved to exit and began filing into the street, the quietness of the night was jolted by a bright flash followed by a loud explosion. Some thought it must be lightening but the sky had cleared revealing a new crescent moon just beginning to be covered in rising smoke. Another blast followed, brighter, louder and nearer than the first. In the distance Keeres could see people running toward them and instinctively flew to meet them. It was Skud and Jojus.

"The square is on fire! The whole place is on fire! They are killing everyone!" Skud shouted without breaking stride.

17

As Darrsce boarded the ship that evening he was filled with mixed emotions. His wife had refused to come with their 5-year-old son, opting instead to stay with her own relations who had likewise chosen the familiar spaces of Maraldia. He would surely miss them and promised to command his own voyage back to Maraldia when he had become well established in Freeland. His father would, of course, never come unless he could bring everything he owned with him. Darrsce did not have a chance to say goodbye to him, nor did he wish it. He imagined only scorn from such an encounter, but Darrsce was determined to prove the wisdom of his move upon his return.

"These will be your quarters for the voyage. Not what you are accustomed to I'm sure but the best this vessel has to offer. Please let me know personally if there is anything you need," Donem commented while escorting Darrsce aboard.

Darrsce nodded appreciatively and closed the door behind him, settling into the small bunk. At least it was a private room unlike the vast majority who slept eight to 10 per berth. After what seemed like an hour of fitful tossing, Darrsce was aroused by what he perceived to be thunder and exited his quarters to go topside. He was met in the stairwell by a sentry.

"Only deckhands topside during the night, Ambassador Darrsce," the sentry informed.

Ambassador, thought Darrsce, *he knows my name and considers me an ambassador*.

The flattery pleased him and gave a certain reassurance that he had made the right decision.

"Tell me, son, is there a storm on the horizon? It seemed to be clear when I went below deck no more than an hour ago, but

I'm sure I heard the roll of thunder," Darrsce played the stately ambassador as he addressed the young man.

"No sir, Ambassador. No storm in sight. But you know the winters in these parts, things can change fast," the sentry soothed.

"But I'm certain I heard thunder," Darrsce rejoined, not easily placated.

"Ship's noise, Ambassador. A ship can make plenty of strange noises in the ears of a man not used to sea going. I'll let you know if anything changes," said the sentry, also playing his role well.

Darrsce turned to go but lingered in the hallway enough to learn that the sentry was changing duty with another and that this new lad regularly moved about on the ship, leaving the stairwell unguarded periodically if Darrsce could time it just right. He observed the stairwell and the feet of the sentry on deck passing by every four minutes for the last half an hour. Next round he would give the sentry 30 seconds to clear the area and then take his look around topside for perhaps a minute before the sentry circled back. At worst, if caught, he could claim ignorance of ship's protocol to the new sentry. He needed to take the chance since he had continued to hear the thunder and had become even more convinced that the first sentry was lying and wanted to know why. Darrsce quietly moved up the steps into the fresh sea air. He could still hear the periodic thunder but the darkness in concert with his Maraldian vision did not afford him anything worth seeing. Then he spotted the Captain's ocuscope and remembered talk of these being a highly powered version of the oculars which Donem demonstrated in the council chambers. He picked them up and put them to his eyes, aiming them toward his native Maraldia about 20 stanion away.

Maraldia in flames!

Darrsce twisted the lenses of the ocuscope to improve the focus as another peel of 'thunder' met his ears preceded by a bright flash from the western suburbs of the city. He watched in horror as smoke and flame rose from every corner of the city. If the ocuscope had been more powerful it would have revealed the city gates now closed by the Freemen to all those who were streaming in from the outside settlements wanting access to the northern passage which was located within the city forest region. All such travelers were now being redirected to the shore or to the firing squad.

"Do you find it interesting?"

Donem surprised Darrsce from behind, and behind Donem the youthful sentry that had first met Darrsce at the stairwell stood, bayonet at the ready.

"What is this monstrous thing, what is this treason?!" Darrsce could not find the words or the breath to vent his emotion and began to feel lightheaded. "My wife and child," he grimaced and turned away from Donem, "my father."

"Your wife and child are safely on their way from the shore, the last ship has been reserved for them. Even your father has been persuaded, though I must say with no little effort," Donem's words gave Darrsce a thread to grasp, keeping him from sinking into complete despair.

"Treason none the less!" Darrsce had regained some of his fighting spirit. "What was all this deception of boundless horizons and brotherhood? Will the charred remains of my countrymen thank you for this kindness?"

"Those who find the passage to the Northern Kingdom will wish a thousand times over that they had burned this night in your city. What awaits them there is surely a fate worse than what you have seen through the ocuscope," there was something about Donem's tone that convinced Darrsce he spoke from his purest belief.

~ 138 ~

But what was this talk of a Northern Kingdom? thought Darrsce.

"So there *is* a northern passage and a city beyond! Donem you have spared no lie in your dealings with me. What bond can we now have? What have you saved us from that could possibly be worse than the violent death of this night?" Darrsce was reeling and could hardly speak.

"Dear Darrsce, I told you what you needed to hear in order to save your life; In order to preserve your people, our people," Donem consoled.

"So we are indeed of the same ancestors, or was that a lie as well?" Darrsce countered and squinted at Donem as though attempting to filter out further deceptions.

"We are. Our common ancestors did not originate in Freeland as I previously described, but in the Northern Kingdom. I apologize for the half-truths delivered to you and the council, it was temporarily necessary. Please listen now to the whole truth. Our ancestors fled that despotic rule more than 5,000 years ago. It is a place of abject slavery. No citizen there is free to do as he wills but must be subject at all times to the will of the King. It is a life worse than death. It is fixed into the fabric of that domain and cannot be altered. Those desiring freedom from this tyranny forcibly commandeered a fleet of ships and set sail as far away as possible. The origins of Maraldia are, as I stated earlier, an accidental colony brought about by an unfortunate tempest," Donem summarized.

"But we are free enough in Maraldia. Why all these extraordinary plans and elaborate webs of deception. Why not leave us be?" Darrsce questioned, he could not understand.

"Because the Lie of the North has now come upon you as he said he would when our ancestors first departed. He will woo each Maraldian into his slavery with promises of peace and prosperity and soon enough from Maraldia stage an attack on

Freeland. You Maraldians will become his fresh troops ready to march upon Freeland. It was decreed by the ancient King and will be attempted. The smell of the north is already rife within your city. We could never have come with entreaties of saving you from an evil northern power while you breathe the winsome air of the wicked lie. The deception is too powerful, it is even laced throughout your ancient myths as I saw in your festival proceedings; glorious "Givers" crushing the evil rebels. That royal line is extremely potent, mark my words your people have long been and are now in great danger. You have heard the song of the girl for yourself. It is the first seed. When the full force of that magic is arrayed none will resist…to their own demise," Donem tensed as he spoke of Selah.

"But haven't you done the same? Promised peace and prosperity?" Darrsce countered.

"The Freemen are not the ones seeking conquest of the North; the North is seeking to come upon *us*. We only wish to be left to our freedom and if bringing our ancient Maraldian brothers along strengthens that end, all the better," Donem's words began to show some earnest emotion.

Darrsce was beginning to believe Donem now that he was confessing something of a selfish motive to the entire endeavor. The mission to Maraldia was a strategic military maneuver at the outset with charitable intent a secondary consideration. The logic and motives began to make sense. And indeed he had heard the song and felt its pull; there was truth in this at least.

Donem's ability to feed Darrsce just enough truth to keep him placated was masterful.

"Then if you consider us partners in your war with the Northern Kingdom, explain the true nature of your voyage to Lered and give him charge over the people and a lead ship. They will follow his direction. Make us your partners to prove that we are not your slaves."

"It is agreeable, though you will need to stand-in for Lered," Donem informed.

"Why? What has happened to Lered?" Darrsce raised his surprised eyes from the deck to see Donem's outstretched arm pointing at the burning Maraldia.

18

Keeres immediately rejoined his departing visitors in the street outside his house.

"Rohon, take five men and go to Noble's shop and gather as many oil lamps as you can carry. The key is under the triangular stone under the rain barrel in the back, or kick in the door if you please. I'll meet you at the old tree in the forest. It is in the very middle, east to west, and only 300 paces from the base of the Tolis. If I am not there within two hours, or if the Freemen are upon you, take everyone through the tunnel," commanded Keeres.

"Who will lead the rest to the tree?" Keeres looked for a leader among the remainder of the group.

"I know the way," an unseen voice spoke from the back of the crowd. The group parted and Skud emerged. He had stopped his flight upon seeing Keeres and his family in the street.

"All right, Skud, lead the way. Locenes, bring only our satchels of water for the group to share. We will need nothing else. Each one of you, do not waste time going back for anything but your kinsmen, and then only if you dare. Make all haste to the tree. Skud, move quickly," Keeres directed.

"But Keeres, where are you going?" Locenes' heart was tearing.

"Noble," he looked her in the eye, "I'll see you at the tree."

Keeres embraced Locenes, burying his face into her neck and then dashed off toward the nearby stables.

As he ran, Keeres saw a city in tumult. Surprised families were coming out of their houses to noise and smoke and shouting.

Freemen were entering houses and ordering people to the ships. Those who refused had their houses set on fire as an incentive and those who forcibly resisted where shot. Disheveled families with crying children were being dragged through the streets. Maraldians who had suspected this affront from the beginning had made meager preparations and assembled militias in various parts of the city doing their best with swords and stones to counter the force of impellors and black powder bombs. Keeres as a lone runner was not a prime target for the advancing Freemen. He made his way to the nearby stables easily enough. Fortunately for him, his daily work in the stables left him both with keys and knowledge of all which he now sought. He saddled the two strongest stallions in the barn, grabbed rope and tackle and headed out toward the jail. A two stanion ride to the jail seemed like 100 as the skittish horses, one being ridden and the other in tow, bucked and bolted at every impellor shot and bomb blast. Burning buildings and Freemen soldiers blocked major roads making what should have been a straight route into a twisted path of side streets and alleyways. At one point, two Freemen soldiers ordered him to halt as he happened upon a busy intersection. He stopped and to their queries replied that he was taking his family to freedom as fast as possible, which garnered their rousing encouragements of "Freedom! Flee to freedom!" as they slapped his stallion's hindquarters through the intersection.

Arriving at the Capitol with the adjoining police station and jail, Keeres noted that the council chamber had been bombed and was engulfed in flames. The entire outer wall had crumbled exposing the ornate interior. Statues of ancient heroes in flames, the elevated council seats as well. Keeres flashed back to that day with the infant Selah seven years earlier and his impassioned plea to the council. His thoughts were interrupted by a Freemen soldier in the square, "You there! Hold your position!"

Keeres stayed put but looked square at the officer, raised his fist to the sky and mimicked the previous officers, "Freedom! Flee to freedom!"

The officer saluted with his raised fist and rejoined "Freedom!" and motioned Keeres on his way.

Keeres made his way around the back of the of the Capitol building jail and up to Noble's barred window saying, "Brother Noble, I have brought the keys!" and flung two ropes through the bars.

"Make haste and tie those to the center bar," he instructed as he affixed pulling collars upon both horses.

In a moment Keeres was whipping the horses into action and the center bar popped out like a rotten tooth. Unfortunately the other six bars and their surrounding bricks were no worse for the wear.

"Quickly again, only try four bars at once!" Keeres instructed.

Maraldian soldiers periodically passed by the nearby cross streets as he impatiently waited for Noble to finish.

"Freedom!" he shouted the magic word with raised fist if their glances lingered too long in his direction.

"Yes, freedom indeed Keeres but why all the shouting? All is ready," Noble questioned, and informed in the same breath.

"I'll explain later," Keeres replied and hurriedly whipped the horses, and they leapt with furious force.

To his surprise, three stories of outer wall collapsed in a heap at his feet. Noble and Keeres stared at each other delightedly stunned and simultaneously shouted "FREEDOM!" with hands thrown up into the air.

However, the noisy commotion of the collapsing wall did not escape the notice of the Freemen soldier in the square and he bolted around back to investigate. As Keeres and Noble finished untying the ropes and collars he turned the back corner and spotted them.

"Stop!" he shouted.

Keeres raised a fist to the sky but this time it was met by an impellor blast.

Further shots rang out as the soldier dashed toward them, now reloading as he came. Keeres and Noble were on the horses in an instant and dashed out of the narrow street in the opposite direction before he could finish.

The horses carried them swiftly through the chaotic square and into an adjoining side street. The scenes before Noble's eyes were more than he could bear as Freemen soldiers burned and killed their way through the city.

Halfway to the edge of the forest, Noble's eye caught a Freemen soldier pulling a young mother by the hair while her two small children squirmed in the arms of two others. Before Keeres knew what was happening Noble rode swiftly by the first officer and kicked him in the face sending him sprawling, out cold. In a flash Noble was off the horse and engaging the other two who had immediately dropped the children and reached for their impellors. Before they could find their target, Noble had broken the arm of one soldier over a nearby hitching post, taken his impellor and, not knowing how to operate it, used it instead as a club upon the head of the second. Before they could recover, Noble had hoisted the young mother and her two children upon his horse. Finally, he mounted himself and bolting away to the snorts of the sweating stallion. Keeres, finding new inspiration from his friend, swung low as he rode and hoisted a fleeing child onto his horse and then a moment later another. Shots and explosions rang out from every direction as they reached the final plaza before the forest. The air was thick with smoke and the whizzing of impellor balls. Apparently the Freemen knew that this spot was a main entrance into the forest and were determined to cut it off.

Noble saving the mother and children

Both horses reached the small gulley separating the cobblestone road from the little meadow leading into the forest and leapt in unison as an impellor blast rang out at point blank range from a Freemen soldier hiding in the gully.

Noble hit the ground with a thud, impellor slug buried in his chest. His horse continued and Keeres slowed just enough to turn and see Noble rise to his knees and shout, "Ride Keeres to true freedom!" before a fresh barrage of impellor fire lay him down again.

The two horses quickly made the cover of the forest where no Freemen had yet pursued and Keeres burst into a heaving sob of grief for his lost brother. The four children and young mother also whimpered and sobbed alternately as the pace slowed through the dark forest lit only by the light of the crescent moon now high in the sky.

"Don't worry, all will be well now," he spoke to reassure his new friends as he stifled his own sobs.

Keeres picked through the forest with sweat and tears streaming down his face and recalled his first journey there with Selah. He suddenly remembered the guiding hand of Rivoas on that journey and immediately looked to the mountain. Just as before, there was Rivoas, this time revealed dimly by flickering firelight. Keeres wondered how he could look so peaceful as he witnessed the destruction of Maraldia and its people. But peaceful he was, and it filled Keeres with a measure of peace as well.

As Keeres broke through the last cluster of brush entering upon the clearing with the ancient tree, his eyes met a sight he had somehow not anticipated.

Thousands and ten thousands of Maraldians crowded the clearing waiting for their turn at the tunnel, with Selah welcoming each one.

19

Skud took charge of the group as Keeres dashed away to the stables. He was a seasoned leader of sorts and his motley gang tagged along with the rest not knowing what else to do. Mrs. Turneur stood gaping at Skud in his tattered attire.

"What er *you* lookin' at? Ya comin' er not?" Skud gave her the same sharp treatment as he would any other.

Locenes bent over to straighten Skud's hair and tidy him up a bit whispering, "You're a fine leader, Skud, this will help you look the part. Take us to the tree."

Locenes encourages Skud

Skud felt embarrassed and excited at the same time as the gentle hands of a loving mother straightened his ragged apparel. She slung two satchels loaded with water casks across his chest. He was not accustomed to such caring treatment from anyone and certainly not an adult female.

"Let's go, I know a better way'an the main roads that the Freemen are gonna take."

Skud lead them down the first alleyway to the west as the Freemen advanced up the street just a few blocks behind them.

As they passed Skud's former house Stohl saw him in front of the determined pack and chased him down the street.

"Skud, you come back here this minute. What's goin' on out here?" Stohl shouted, trying to catch up.

Stohl's normal slurry of abuses were muted due to the numerous eyes that followed him. He quickly made his way to Skud at the front of the pack.

"Son, you tell me now what's goin' on here," Stohl whispered while Skud continued his steady unchecked pace.

"Son? When were the last time you call me *son*? We're goin' to the mountain and I suggest you do the same. Unless you wanna go to the boats, er die in yer house," Skud's eyes remained fixed on the road ahead as he spoke.

"You goin' to the mountain in the middle of the night? Come on back to the house, you kin live with me ag'in."

Stohl sensed the palpable fear that was in the air and thought it safer to regain his old roommate.

Just then a blast a half a stanion behind them shook the street. Everyone instinctively crouched, glancing behind to see the entire way they had just traversed engulfed in a wall of flame.

"Ya got three choices, pops, take yer pick. We's goin' to the mountain."

~ 149 ~

Skud did not say any more. Stohl fell in behind the rest of the group, darting his eyes to and fro at every unexpected noise and movement. He reasoned that he could always come back to his loot when the commotion was over.

The rest of the walk to the tree went as smoothly as could be imagined under the circumstances. Selah entertained those within earshot with stories of her travels to the mountain a few days before, feeling very much like Noble describing his adventures. She seasoned this commentary with description of Rivoas, now standing in the cave of the mountain bathed in firelight. Her words encouraged the group and those on the outer edges wished they were closer and could hear every detail.

Arriving in the clearing they were surprised to see several thousand already there but only a few dared enter the underground tunnel for lack of light. Soon Rohon arrived with his men carrying two dozen lanterns.

"It was every light in the shop," Rohon informed the group with a shrug. "We'll light them all and stage them every few hundred paces throughout the tunnel."

Rohon and his men quickly went to work as word spread that the little girl with the song had arrived. Selah quickly became a celebrity as everyone wished to pat her on the head or give her the traditional slight bow of the head and flowing half arm extension typical among the formal. It was almost a merry mood there in the forest as people waited for the lanterns to be arranged.

"All is ready. Selah, I believe you should be the first," Rohon directed and wiped the sweat from his brow at the entrance to the tunnel.

Someone had already dug steps from ground level into the soil and reinforced each with tightly fitted branches, enabling easier access to the underground passage.

"I want to wait for Papa!" Selah implored to her mother, and Locenes responded with a nod.

"Skud, you lead the way. You have been here before and your vision is best," Locenes suggested.

The plan suited them all and into the tunnel went Skud with a stream of thousands behind him. The tunnel seemed a much cheerier place to Skud than the first time through, lit as it was with Noble's lanterns, and the journey passed much quicker.

"Welcome back, my son!" The bright smile of Rivoas greeted him as he turned the last corner into the cave opening where the fire was dancing.

The word "son" impressed itself on Skud's mind as he glanced over his shoulder to see Stohl a few heads behind. The fragrant smell of Rivoas' mountain passage brightened his eyes as he entered fully into the cave mouth. The panorama before him was beautiful and appalling all at once.

Maraldia in flames, a throng of souls crowding the forest, and an armada of ships in the moonlight making their final preparations completed the view.

"Quickly now, all has been provided. Mount this steed, he knows where to go," were the only additional words given by Rivoas.

Skud was amazed at the size and beauty of this animal, slightly bigger than any he had seen in Maraldia and with an expression of intelligence in its eye. He mounted quickly and without hesitation the animal charged headlong into the mountain passage. The passage was lit by torches hung high upon the walls and Skud wondered how one man could have made such preparations. An endless queue of like colored stallions, pure white, assembled to his left as far down the passage as the eye could see, awaiting their riders as he plunged along on the right.

Skud's exhilaration at such a ride soon gave way to sleepiness as the sweet mountain air soothed his nerves and the soft mane of the stallion gave rest to his head. He fell asleep and the stallion, with remarkable agility, sensed the change and adjusted its gait constantly to balance the boy perfectly as he rested.

Skud awoke some time later not knowing if he had slept an hour or a week and would have been astonished to know just how long it had truly been. Within sight was the awaited opening of the fragrant mountain passage, bright midday sun streaming in. As he arrived and slid to the ground his faithful mount nuzzled against the side of his head and Skud could have sworn it whispered softly and deeply into his ear, "Choose well," but wrote it off as the lingering phantoms of his extended dreaming. The horse trotted out of the passageway and into a bright lush meadow to refresh itself on the clover. In the distance across the meadow Skud could clearly see an enormous city surrounded by a high wall with shining granite slab gates facing east toward a large lake with forest beyond, high mountains climbing higher and higher in the distance.

Presently others joined Skud, and their horses followed the lead of the first. At first they were mostly members of Skud's gang interspersed by various followers, including Stohl. A bright one like Rivoas, except female, stood to the right of the passage exit and motioned for Skud to enter into what looked like a hole just wide enough for one in a spot where the cave wall met the floor.

"Welcome! All who wish to enter the city must go this way," the bright one directed.

She was the most beautiful woman Skud had ever seen, tall with long straight hair to her waist and a face that could hold spellbound the coldest heart.

He stood for a moment forgetting the strangeness of the entire situation then recovered, "Ain't that the Northern Kingdom right there?" he questioned pointing to the city in the distance.

"It is indeed. And a marvelous city it is. Come this way to enter," the bright one again motioned to the narrow hole.

"What kind'a horse mess is that? I can see the city right there across this here wide field. I can walk there in an hour," Stohl taunted, "You some kind'a liar? You want to kill us all, pushin' us into some dark skinny hole in the ground?"

"You cannot get to the city that way. Come, a way has been prepared. It is the *only* way," the bright one countered.

"I come all this way already and now just this wide easy rollin' field be between me and that city. You a liar if ever there were a liar, and a bad liar too. Come'on Skud let's git across this here field before all these other folks come and take the best spots," Stohl coerced.

Skud glanced at Stohl and the city in the distance then back to the bright one.

"Come on Skud, let's go with your dad. It's not very far," Jojus joined in.

Skud glanced around again and without a word bolted for the hole and threw himself in feet first. The stunned crowd stood in shock as they heard his screams echoing away into the depths below.

20

When it was all said and done only slightly more than half of the Maraldians boarded the ships, still a sizable number around 250,000. Only about 10,000 made it to the tree. The rest were either slaughtered or being hunted down as the ships began to head south that seventh festival day.

Darrsce was given command over the portion of the fleet which carried the Maraldians and manned the decks with experienced Maraldian sailors. However, all weapons were transferred to the remaining Freemen ships; Darrsce could negotiate nothing better. The Freemen ships prepared to weigh anchor escorting both behind and to the sides of Darrsce and his new armada.

As the sun began to illuminate the eastern sky less than 1,000 Maraldians were still waiting their turn at the tunnel. Rohon had convinced Keeres to take his family through the tunnel midway through the night; he would stay until the last had passed through. Locenes thanked Rohon for that courtesy and as the small family approached the steps to the tunnel everyone stood to watch, applaud, and whistle their gratitude.

Keeres hoisted Selah to his shoulders so she could see and said, "I don't think ***these*** people are laughing at you."

Selah wept.

The rising sun had also given new courage to the spent Freemen soldiers and as the battles within the city quieted they made their way to the forest. Darkness had hindered their entrance until now, being that no Freemen had ever actually seen a forest and the thought of entering one during the night was more than the bravest of them could bear. Emboldened by the sun, Freemen troops began to enter the forest following trails that the escaping Maraldians had cut.

As the last few hundred Maraldians made their way into the tunnel, the Freemen soldiers neared the clearing. Rohon had anticipated this moment and had posted scouts to provide advanced warning. The warning had come 15 minutes ago and his men took their positions scattering 100 paces deep into the forest around the entire perimeter of the clearing lying in wait, though they had only spears and stones to aid their attack. The Freemen were nonetheless surprised as these meager weapons were thrust upon them from behind every rock and tree as they neared the clearing. Some Freemen, still fearful of the forest, turned and fled. Others battled on as the last of the Maraldians were given the time to hurry into the tunnel.

"Fffsssseeeeooooeeee!" Rohon put his fingers to his mouth to whistle the signal for his improvised army to make for the tunnel. All others were safely in and now it was only these brave men left, half of whom had fallen to Freemen impellors in the forest while allowing the others to escape. Rohon saw the last man dive for the tunnel and sprinted from the cover of the forest.

PANG! And twice more, PANG! PANG! Impellor shots rang through the clearing.

Rohon was hit in the leg and back but was still stumbling toward the tunnel opening. A Freemen soldier darted from the forest and tackled him full speed taking both of them to the ground. Rohon still had some fight left in him and was upon the back of the soldier in a second choking him with one arm and pounding his head with the other fist.

"This one is for Selah!"

POW!

"This one is for Keeres!"

POW! He pummeled the soldier.

PANG! PANG! Rohon slumped over in a heap as dozens of Freemen soldiers, impellors drawn, entered the clearing.

"Into the tunnel!" shouted the Freemen commander.

Freemen soldiers began entering the tunnel but the fragrance flowing down from the passage of Rivoas filled the tunnel and was to them as the stench of rotting flesh. They coughed and swore and covered their faces. The commander cursed them on but even those with the mettle to pursue soon fell, poisoned by the northern breeze.

"To the ships!" the commander ordered as he saw the hopelessness of further pursuit. "Kill anyone you find on the way out."

And so they did. Though there were not many left to find, so thorough was the initial Freemen assault. Similar scenes were playing out in every Maraldian settlement up and down the coast. A few Maraldians even now turned from these settlements to the shore if the Freemen would still allow, seeing the futility of any other choice. By the time the sun dipped below the horizon that seventh festival day, the last foot had stepped from shore to ship. The last dying breath was passed.

Maraldia was no more.

21

"Whud I tell ya! That boy ain't no son o'mine! Dang fool! Dead is dead, an' he dead. Dumb stupid rebel child! You all better now come along with me!" Stohl berated Skud and threw up his hands as Skud's cries from the underground cavern dwindled away.

The rest of the gang just stood dumbfounded. Presently a very aged gentleman tottered over to the bright one. He was bent with years and shuffled along slowly but with purpose.

"What's down there?" he inquired of the bright one in a voice weak and spent.

"It is the way, as I have said. All who wish to enter the city must pass through," came the reply.

"It don't make much sense to me, ya know," the old man muttered in a low voice as he struggled to twist his stiff stooped frame enough to get a single glassy eye on the face of the tall bright one.

"Must it?" the bright one answered with a question.

"Ohhhh dang it," whimpered the frustrated old man as he tottered over to the hole, sat himself down on the edge and slipped effortlessly away.

"Woooohoooo!" came the soft fading aged echo from the cavern entrance.

The old man questions the bright one

"Now don't that beat all! Young fools and old fools alike! I'm not stayin' here another minute. Who's with me?" Stohl sifted the gathering crowd.

"There is a way that seems right to man, but in the end leads to death," the bright one countered Stohl.

"Yer dang riddles already lead to the death o' my boy!" Stohl fumed. "Who's with me?"

By this time a fair number of horse and riders had been deposited in the spot and many had watched the disappearance of Skud and the old man. Stohl gathered a small cadre from that brood who wanted nothing to do with narrow ways and headed off for the city across the meadow. They found the going a bit tougher than they imagined, for between the mountain passage and the city there were steep ravines and fast flowing rivers, unseen from their initial vantage point.

Nevertheless, they pressed on as did several other small groups after them.

Not many days later, the old man would recount his experience through the narrow way as all who entered the Northern Kingdom loved to do.

"I seemed to fall a long time, so long in fact that the initial fear of falling subsided. I began to make efforts to fall in a dignified manner. *If I must fall, let it not be with tumbling and flailing of arms*, I thought to myself," the old man smiled at his audience as he spoke.

"That's very amusing, I just flopped around like a rag doll in a wind storm!" remarked a young girl.

"Yes, even then I was concerned about appearances. Can you imagine such a thing? In any case I was more or less successful in my attempts, though I expected to be dashed to pieces momentarily at the bottom of the pitch black cavern," the old man continued.

"It wasn't pitch black for me!" interjected one young man, "I could see everything but in colors like I'd never seen before!"

"You can tell your story next," chided the young man's mother, who looked no older than him. "Go on, please," she motioned to the old man.

"Well, instead of a sudden crashing at the bottom of the cavern I seemed to be 'caught' as though the air itself was getting thicker and gently slowing my fall. The slowing continued until I perceived that I was no longer falling but instead being carried along in what seemed to be a forward direction like in a current, though honestly I could not tell you what was forward, backward, up or down in that place. Then the light, the searing blinding light."

"Yes, yes, the light. It was the same for me," came the acknowledgement from all his listeners.

Each story was different in its particulars, but some elements were always the same.

He continued, "I closed my eyes and screamed in pain, thinking I would surely be incinerated. My eyelids were no match for this light because no matter what I did, the brightness penetrated. The light seemed to come from somewhere in front of me but strangely enough I could feel its effect even on my back, and stranger still even on my inner organs. The light felt like an antiseptic on a dirty wound, but in this case my whole body was the wound."

Nodding heads confirmed a common experience for all.

"I crumpled myself into a ball in an attempt to escape the sensation, but it was to no avail. I could see nothing and wondered if I'd been blinded. The light did its work for only a few seconds, but they were memorable seconds. The burning subsided and I straightened up to the happy discovery that my sight was restored. Not only that, but I felt like I was 25 again… but better somehow, strong and full of fight."

"The body renewed!" the crowd shouted in unison, as became the custom for all such recounting.

"Yes, indeed," the old man replied, smiling and raising one hand to the sky. "I continued to float through some kind of medium like water which was substantial enough to suspend me, but at the same time I seemed to be breathing it."

"Wow, that's a lot different than what happened to me next," the young man could not contain himself but then caught the eye of the others and again quieted.

The old man grinned and went on, "To my surprise I was not in a place that looked like a closed in cavern at all but instead like the most wide open place you could imagine. It was like flying through a blue cloudless sky without a planet below to give orientation of up or down. It was then that I realized I was naked."

Everyone smiled shyly, each remembering their own moment of realization.

"But it wasn't the nakedness that made me feel uncomfortable because a new sensation was now upon me. It seemed as though my emotion, will, and intellect took visible shapes before my eyes. These three dominant actors of my soul came to me, and they were hideous creatures," the old man spoke with great passion and paused momentarily to compose himself.

"What I instinctively knew should be sleek and beautiful forms were dark, twisted and contorted. Bulging features where slender curves should have been and leanness where there should have been substance. I was alarmed to see myself in this new truest light, and I was ashamed."

"We have all seen the same of ourselves," someone from the back spoke for all.

"Before I had time to despair something like a bolt of lightning split the space between me and them. They were charred and writhed in pain. I pitied them. But almost immediately their burned outer skins peeled away revealing forms somewhat improved. This cycle repeated many times until the pathetic figures were transformed into majestic winged creatures, beautiful to behold and mighty in power. They flew to me with great speed and I instinctively reached for them like the reunion of a long lost love, and reunited we were."

"The soul renewed!" shouted the crowd in usual form, tears apparent among many.
He went on, "Feeling better with each breath I perceived a dark spot in the steady field of blue in which I was being carried

along. At first I thought it was a nearby speck that I could crush between my fingers but after many minutes of gliding and watching its steady growth, I determined it must be a thing of great size indeed.

"I had hoped that as the object neared, its form would become clearer to me, but in truth it was the opposite. The thing that came into view was so different to anything in my experience, I'm not sure I can make you understand."

"Go on, we will understand," spoke a wise looking gentleman, not looking up from the ornate figurine he was whittling from a small branch.

"Well yes, of course you will," the old man remembered that all his hearers had been through something similar. "It was a marvelous creature, not unlike a man in form but then again nothing like a man. See, it is hard to explain."

"Go on," said the wise gentleman.

"Well to begin with, the creature was enormous. Ten times the size of our Maraldian Capitol building, I was still two stanion away and could view it most clearly. In addition to sheer size the creature seemed to occupy more space than actually existed. I mean he moved in a direction for which I have no word. Not up or down, north or south, east or west. Maybe 'in' and 'out' are the best I can do, but even that is poor. In and out of what? The world itself? I cannot say. He was able to twist into himself in a way that I thought must damage his internal organs, if he had any, but he was none the worse. He seemed to possess more sides than were physically possible, does that make any sense?"

"There are ears to which it does, go on." The figurine was almost complete.

"Well, this creature was dark and withered and wore a burial shroud. I thought it strange that such a marvelous creature should be in a burial shroud as though it were dead. Its eyes darted to and fro as though in search of something it had lost, but seemed to have no ability to find. It did nothing but search, or sat in despair as long as I watched. I wondered how long it had been searching."

"Since the day of its undoing, most certainly," the wise gentleman interjected, picking a bit of material away from the carving.

"Then, as it sat, I began to notice something peculiar. I raised my arms above my head to stretch and noticed that the creature did the same. Then I straightened my legs in front of me and reached for my toes. Again the creature did the same in its own 'in and out' way of moving. I could not discern if he mimicked me or I mimicked him."

"Yes, I know what happens next!" said the young man.

"Yes, perhaps it was the same for all of us at this point. The creature looked directly at me and spoke. It alarmed me very much to have such a giant address me. However, as he spoke I could feel his very words coming up from within me, as though I were the one speaking, 'Though I am imperceptible to eyes of flesh, you are my visible projection into realms of soil and air. You are my stallion, but I cannot ride. I am your guide, but my sextant is broken. I am your spirit, and I am dead.' The creature finished his address to me with slumped head and shoulders."

The youth stared with open mouth, finally speechless.

"Then suddenly the creature looked up into the distance and I felt his heart, my heart, rise in anticipation. He stood just in time to see a meteor split the sky, coming from the direction for which I have no word. It spoke with the voice of the one who had come to Selah but was suddenly and violently destroyed in flight, bursting into innumerable pieces, showering the giant with a flood of red. I felt his burial shroud melt away under the cleansing of that shower to reveal a shining robe. His withered frame became a bulwark. I sensed a transformation akin...I can only liken it, to birth."

"And so it must be," said the wise one, looking straight at the old man for the first time.

"Then the most peculiar sensation came upon me. It may be likened to the feeling of a new soldier when first meeting his swarthy commander. There was awe and respect, mixed with a measure of fear. I greatly wished, with body and soul, to follow the lead of this shining star; to gladly follow his every impulse. With irresistible joy I flung myself upon him, felt myself painfully but happily stretched to his dimensions, and we became one fluid being.

"The spirit renewed! The soul renewed! The body renewed!" shouted the crowd in unison.

Back in the present, as Stohl set out with his raggedy band on his trek across the meadow, the old man was already surfacing from beneath the waters of the lake in front of the Northern Kingdom gate. The entire transformation had only taken a moment, though for him it seemed much longer. Upon his first stroke toward the shore he recognized something different. Instead of the decrepit old joints of an 87 year old man, his well-muscled arms easily pulled him through the water. As he climbed out he caught his reflection in the water and saw not a wrinkled old face but the face he had not seen in the mirror for more than 60 years! The tunic he was wearing had not a spot or tear and fit perfectly as he leapt and thrust his fist into the air.

"Calm down old man, the best is yet to come," cracked the handsome bearded man without looking up as he sat next to the fire on the beach.

"Skud, is that you?" the old man spoke in surprise.

"Well who do you think went in the hole before you?" The transformation had not burned the wise guy out of Skud.

Then Skud leapt from the fire and pounced on the old man with a great laugh and they wrestled in the grass, the old man rejoicing in his strength and getting the best of Skud. They fell away from each other laughing and sweating like children.

22

The reunion on the beach grew moment by moment and every new face that sprung from the lake was like the first day of the festival, full of surprise, joy and excitement; as though each one watching was receiving a personal gift with every new appearance. Shouts and laughter and welcomes thundered all around at each new splashing.

"Lered! Dear Lered! Ha ha!"
"Velcer! Oh Velcer!"
"Ho hooo! It is Mrs. Turneur!"

And of course the reception for Selah and her family was exceptional as each person expressed gratitude for the channel through which the message came. Skud in particular was remarkably taken with the beauty of the now full grown Selah, tall and fully figured with long dark wavy hair flowing over her shoulders framing her green eyes and innocent smile like an exquisite picture frame encasing an artistic masterpiece.

"Skud, may I have a brief word with you?" a tall bright eyed man with neatly trimmed beard questioned.

"Excuse me sir, do I know you?" Skud searched the intelligent face for some recollection.

"Ha, Skud! It is Kwea! How soon you have forgotten your old cohort, your means to obtain Maraldian ale!" Kwea turned his head down and to the side a bit and gave half a squint, pretending to be slighted.

"Kwea? I'm sorry, your manner is so much changed. Your expression is sharp and full of whit!"

Then realizing that his words might be perceived as an insult followed up, "I mean, we all are so changed!"

"I understand, Skud. In truth, it is I who wished to apologize to you. I killed you a thousand times in my heart back in Maraldia. With every slight or insult, I killed you afresh. Will you forgive me?" Kwea looked to the ground.

Silence.

Skud stared at Kwea with a lump in his throat. When he could muster the composure to speak he said, "Kwea, you show yourself to be a better man than I once again. I forgive and ask the same of you."

Kwea looked up with a grin and said, "Thank you, of course."

They shook hands and embraced, something never thought of in all their years together in Maraldia. Then Skud twisted the embrace into a headlock and Kwea returned a punch to the ribs as they parted with a smile.

About the time the last person was bubbling up from the lake, Selah saw Rivoas walking toward the crowd from the direction of the city gate. She ran to him across the soft grass and oh, how she could run; how they all could run! She was surprised that he no longer looked exceptionally bright or in super focus as she remembered. But it was not because he was any bit the lesser; it was because each of them had become the more.

They walked and talked and as all assembled, he addressed them, his voice booming over the thousands "See the city of which you are citizens. It is the city from which all life comes. There *is* an existence apart from life and it is called death. Some have called it by other names and freely chosen this existence, until they become unable to choose anything else."

He paused for a moment and Selah thought his eyes had become wet, then continued, "You are a part, not the whole. You are a lively stream, but not the headwater. You were created for a joyfully dance, choreographed to your lover's perfect melody, not a song of your own making. It was never intended for you to be your own ultimate master; there is no possible design that can work that way. Some from this country, long ago, thought this order of things a bondage too great to bear and brought treason upon the King. These were expelled; it was the only mercy left for those with damaged eyes which could no longer bear the brightness of the city. They were given ships in which to sail and sail they did, infecting other dominions of the King with their blindness as they went. Therefore the King caused a great wind to blow such that their ships would be driven far out to sea, and caused a great stone to rise from the ground to shelter his damaged dominions from the winds until the appointed time of their healing. That time is has come. There, I have told you. Now come into the endless city."

As he finished, Stohl and his small battalion crested their final hill and joined the assembly. They were haggard and disheveled from the difficult journey but proud of their accomplishment.

"Father!" exclaimed Skud as he ran to meet him.

"Who is you?" Stohl replied with contempt, though feeling somewhat puny in the company of such a young and robust looking party.

"I am your son, Skud," replied the grown Skud.

Stohl twisted up his face and squinted his eyes as the resemblance began to dawn on him. "If you is Skud tell me where I hide my money."

"Father, the little money you have is always hidden under the corner floor board nearest the front door," Skud proved his authenticity.

"You stealin' my money, boy?" Stohl accepted the recognition. "What happened to you, all growed up? You think you better'n me? I taken the hard way and lead all these here folks wit me, carrin' em on my back nearly. You done nothing but jump in a dang hole an now you think you better'n me? Dang fool rebel child!"

"No father, not better in the least, though I used to think so," Skud replied.

"Used to think so, did ya? All the while under my roof, eatin' my food, soaking up my heat. Fool rebel child!" Stohl continued.

"Yes I was," Skud admitted.

"Well now we's here, let's git'er on in. Open the gates!" Stohl exulted as best he could.

"I'm afraid you must go back through the narrow way. It is not too late for you even now," Rivoas interrupted.

"Go back all that way?" Stohl paused and spoke softer, "Even though now I kin see it dun ya some good," Stohl at least admitted the obvious in quiet tones before again raising his voice, "It ain't fer me. I don't need no fixin' up. Open the dang gate." He was defiant.

Some of Stohl's motley entourage did in fact start back to the mountain passage seeing now the plain result before their eyes of entering through the narrow hole, but others bet their money on Stohl.

"You may have it as you wish, as all eventually do, but you will not like it," Rivoas counseled.

"You an'yer dang riddles. I'm a plain talkin' man, and I says I'll like it well enough. Let's go," Stohl made a ridiculous picture, strutting proudly toward the gate looking like a whipped rat amidst the throng of humble nobility.

They all followed behind Stohl, even Rivoas, until they reached the gate. It was a longer walk than they imagined for the wall and gate were enormous, like a far mountain that you think you will easily reach in a moment but which requires an hour's hike.

As they neared, Rivoas approached the massive gate slabs of bright glistening blue granite, knelt down on one knee, placed one hand on the gates, bowed his head and spoke softly, "I have brought your children home."

At his words the gigantic slabs of granite began to fold inward toward the city and pure warm golden light streamed out between them.

Stohl and his team attempted to cover their eyes but did not even have time to utter a single shriek. For them it was like being thrown into the heart of the sun. They were all incinerated in an instant.

For the rest it was as though they could see for the first time, such was the nature of this new light. It was as though they had lived their entire lives by the light of the stars alone, and now the sun had risen to reveal true color and detail. The city reached up into an infinite atmosphere and seemed to reveal broader vistas as it rose. All features of that city became more complex and ornate, larger and brighter the higher the ascent. In fact this gated entrance was the gutter of the Kingdom by comparison to even the next layered tier. Those from the city of orphans were orphaned no more.

The travelers gazed into the light and from within the walls of the city they were greeted by another royal assembly.

"Rohon!" Keeres shouted. "You have always been one to take short cuts now haven't you?" Keeres was quick to renew their old banter.

"Noble!" Selah spotted him first and ran to meet him. "Father said you were lost but I knew you must be here! You have finally made it to the unexplored north! Shall you winter here?" she laughed and joked. "Please, do tell me what these ropes and hooks are for? May I have some shortbread?"

"Ha! You may have better treats than shortbread and I shall tell you great stories indeed, and you shall tell me! I believe there are more adventures here than either of us can exhaust," Noble overflowed with joy.

In addition to these, all those who set out for the mountain passage were among the greeters. Every fighter in the forest and every traveler murdered outside the walls of Maraldia and every seeker whose life was ended by the Freemen was there. Even Skud's lame puppy friend was among them, limber and mended.

Rivoas ushered them all in as they continued their happy discussions, and he fixed the gates so that they would never be closed again.

23

Five months of hard sailing had left all the Maraldians, most of whom had never been on the ocean for more than an afternoon, understandably fatigued. Fortunately there were plenty of provisions since only half of the intended passengers had actually boarded the ships. Darrsce appointed able captains over each ship and they ordered their vessels well so Darrsce had few worries; though the fact that his entire armada had become spread over the ocean by more than half a day's good sailing played on his mind at times. He wished to have them all within ocuscope range.

"Tell me, Donem, is degraded vision one of the side effects of extended exposure to the sea? I can't seem to focus nearly so well as I once did," Darrsce inquired as he peered through the ocuscope for his distant ships.

His unaided vision was in fact less than half the acuity as in Maraldia, perhaps no more than ten paces of clarity. If he had bothered to ask he would have found the same to be true for all who made the southern journey, Freemen and Maraldian alike.

"I have not heard it told," replied Donem, "perhaps you are just getting old, dear friend. I will roust you up some oculars shortly."

Donem and Darrsce had indeed become fast friends these last months with little else to do except tell stories and speculate on their future prospects.

"Another thing I have noticed. Perhaps it is because the winters in Freeland are so different than the northern region, but I observe that the variation between day and night is not nearly so distinct as I am used to," Darrsce queried.

"Ah yes! This is one of the beauties of Freeland. Day and night are nearly the same thing. It is never too bright, and never too dark," Donem was proud to exposit on one of what he perceived to be the many benefits of living in Freeland. "Some would call it perpetual twilight, the very best part of the day at all times!

"And you will find it always temperate. A light coat is usually recommended. Never the dreaded snows that I hear you sometimes get and certainly never the oppressive heat and sun to sap your energy, the persistent cloud cover will make sure of that," Donem boasted.

Darrsce did not speak, but wondered if he had been wrong all these years to enjoy a bright hot summer day or a moonlit winter night in a snow covered forest.

"We have just passed the outer islands and should arrive within two days. You will soon see for yourself," Donem reassured.

Two days later, Darrsce disembarked at the port in Ichabod, the capital city of Freeland. Upon his first sighting of the land through the ocuscope more than two stanion offshore, Darrsce began to get a knot in his stomach. He was not seeing the glistening metropolis he expected.

"Where are the structures, the buildings, the public squares?" Darrsce inquired of Donem, stepping down the gangplank and choking back the panic that was rising within him.

Nowhere in sight was there a single building or fountain, a road or a park. Only stumps of trees and hard packed soil.

"Well first of all, Darrsce, please put on these oculars as all do here in Freeland," Donem calmed.

Darrsce strapped the device across his face and indeed this brand of ocular improved his meager vision 20 fold, though he disliked being dependent on such a fragile contraption.

~ 173 ~

But the view was not much improved.

"Thank you, Donem, but my question still stands," Darrsce reiterated.

"Come this way, the grand city is like none you have ever seen."

Darrsce followed, along with the murmuring captains from the first ten ships to arrive in the port of Ichabod, each donning a pair of oculars. The next contingent of ships would arrive within two hours so these men would need to make a quick assessment and unload their ships in time to make way for the coming fleet.

Donem's excitement at being back on his home soil was beginning to show. Donem led Darrsce and the captains to a railing 300 paces up the steeply inclined dirt path from the port. The view there was appalling and Darrsce was momentarily speechless.

The city of Ichabod was essentially an enormous hole in the ground. An "inverted" city, as it were. There were buildings and roads enough but they all layered down and down again farther and farther away as far as the eye could see. Each building exterior was carved out of the gray stone beneath the gray topsoil and the interiors were reinforced with timber from forests leveled long ago. Flat spaces were designed in various spots to grow the roots and beans that were staples of the Freemen diet. Each building had a water collection system for the infrequent rains but the city was for the most part a desert. Massive elevating platforms powered by a loud and smoky engine constantly lifted people up and down the 45 degree angle to the various levels. The smoke settled in the bottom of the city making Darrsce wonder how anyone could live at the lower levels. It appeared that the city was populated to no more than half its capacity and Darrsce did not observe any interactions between the people he saw. Only Freemen hurriedly going on their way to attend whatever urgent business might crowd their schedule that day. No one had been at the docks to welcome them and it would appear that the great interest in the Maraldian exploration that Donem had alluded to must have been replaced by other pressing concerns.

Donem and Darrsce looking down into Ichabod

"It is amazing, is it not? See how unlimited freedom works! No man must answer to another and all are free to ally or divide as they chose. If one man becomes excessively troublesome, a few will ally for a time to kill him or drive him away. Our government makes no judgments about the rightness of our citizens actions since at our core we believe there is no such thing as ultimate right or wrong, except for the ultimate freedom of the individual," Donem was waxing poetic.

To illustrate, Donem pulled his impellor from its holster, pointed it at an old man passing by one level below the rail and shot him in the back of the head, dead.

"See my freedom at work! I believe this old man is a burden to the entire system here in Freeland, contributing little. I am free to act as I see fit. Is this not exceedingly efficient?" Donem regaled in the smoldering air of his homeland.

Darrsce and the captains stood agape.

"Our ruling council has little work or worry since each man is free to do what is right in his own eyes. Rarely do we have wars because to have a war would mean many coming together for a single cause. Our system of government encourages each man to be a cause unto himself; though for the Maraldian expedition a clear and present danger brought us together, such threats are now over.

"The world is open to you, Darrsce. Unload your people and take whatever residences you can find, there are plenty open here in the capital city alone and there are many such cities throughout Freeland, though not all as grand as this!"

Donem handed Darrsce his due reward.

"Your point is well made," Darrsce said little but thought much. "Now my captains and I will attend to the people."

When Darrsce and the 10 captains returned to the docks, they ferried quickly over to the lead ship for a conference.

"Good men of Maraldia," Darrsce began, "I am emboldened to speak for all since I know each well enough. As you have seen with your own eyes, what lay before us here in Freeland is not what any had supposed. It is a place of anarchy. A gray withered land of lawlessness. I am convinced by a half hour on its shores that I would rather die on the sea than live in this place. If none of you will join me then I will dive into the ocean and swim as far as I can, such is my resolve." Darrsce's tone was flat as a man condemned to die.

Ten sober captains stared at Darrsce, each in complete and despairing agreement.

"If we attempt to leave, it will be considered an act of war against Freeland. Their ships carry all the weapons. We have ships full of women and children. Only with great fortune will any of our fleet clear the outer islands intact, much less endure five more months on the sea," Darrsce continued, the picture not getting any better as he talked.

More silence.

"Your words ring truer to me than any word I ever forced myself to believe about this place," admitted Barve, one of the 10, the scales finally falling completely from his eyes.

"I would rather see my young ones drown in the sea than live in this hole," Gourace, another captain, agreed.

All the rest nodded the same.

Darrsce then caught sight of Donem not 50 paces away on the pier as he glanced momentarily out the cabin door. He was standing with Darrsce's father and both wore an unusual grin as Donem and Darrsce locked eyes.

"Not thinking about leaving are we, Darrsce? See, your father has found Freeland to be a most pleasant place," Donem smirked as he spoke and motioned for Darrsce to look to the left and right of his ships.

Freemen vessels were just anchoring along the shoreline up and down both sides of the Maraldian vessels in the tight harbor of Ichabod. Donem had been thinking of this scenario all along. Certainly the Freemen vessels would be ready for any runners.

Only now did Donem drop all pretenses, and spoke with putrid sarcasm, "What shall the King of the North do now, Darrsce? Will he rescue the puny Maraldian creatures for which he cares so much? Will he send a child to sing you a song?" Donem mocked.

Darrsce's self-imposed blindness completely melted away as the first genuine words from Donem's mouth fell about his ears.

The entire enterprise had never been about the Maraldians, per se, never about Maraldia becoming the staging area for an assault from the north. Darrsce thought. *It had always been about the Freemen seeking some measure of revenge on the King of the North. Settling old scores or at least wounding the adversary to whatever degree possible. There was never the slightest kind intent, never the least bit of brotherly love. All a charade to remove the people, on whom the ancient King apparently had some claim, to a maximum distance from his realm, or to destroy those that could not be removed.*

Darrsce pulled the captains back together momentarily only to say, "There is no disguise, they are ready for us."

There were only a few moments to discuss a run for open water to warn the next wave of the massive fleet now only an hour distant, and Gourace took the lead.

"The Freemen have the weapons, but on the water we have sheer numbers. How can we use this resource to our tactical advantage?" Gourace challenged the seasoned captains.

Ravol, the captain of the lead ship number on which Darrsce traveled with his family observed in reply, "There are only three armed Freemen escort ships with us now, one to our east, one to the west, and one to the north at the mouth of the harbor."

Barve ventured a plan, "I am moored next to the western Freemen vessel. I believe I can lure their captain to my ship with a ruse. When I do, we will have 100 able men ready to take control of their well armored vessel. They are manned with no more than 40.   Ravol, you will need to begin disembarking number one as though all is well. Can you do that amid the stench of this place?"

"I can hold my breath long enough," Ravol replied.

Barve continued, "Gourace, you must play the same ruse as I with the Freemen vessel to the east.   Once successful, we can both make a stealthy approach aboard our newly acquired Freemen vessels to their third ship at the mouth of the harbor. Our 10 Maraldian vessels must be quick to follow.   At that point our intent will be obvious and each must run as best they can. Gourace and I will do our best to clear your path with the captured Freemen ships.   But we must make due haste, there will be many ships clogging the harbor entrance within the hour."

"Understood," Gourace felt a surge of life return to him at the prospect of escape.

"Ravol, begin disembarkation of your ship immediately, and with a smile if you please.   We wish to raise no undue suspicion and it would be best to appear pleased with our new home. Darrsce, can you assist Ravol? Your presence on the pier until the last possible moment will help cover our intentions," Barve directed and questioned all at once.

"I shall make a good show of it indeed," Darrsce rejoined.

"Gourace, come with me," Barve instructed.

A short conference between Gourace and Barve ensued as they improvised a plan to take the Freemen ships that boxed them in to the east and west. A few moments later identical scenes played out a stanion apart on either end of the line of ships as Ravol's ship disembarked directly in the middle.

"Captain, can you assist me with a troublesome situation?" Gourace called across the 20 paces of water between he and the eastern Freemen vessel.

"What is it?" replied the Freemen captain, somewhat irritated to be summoned.

"Darrsce, my commander, has ordered that my vessel be the last of our first 10 ships to disembark. I am the senior captain among us all and clearly deserve to be among the first. Please sir, how should such disputes be handled in Freeland? Can you offer any wise council?" Gourace baited the Freemen.

"Do as you wish stupid Maraldian! This is the only law of our land!" the Freemen captain laughed Gourace to scorn.

Gourace, however, continued to woo the Freemen captain and he guessed a thick flattery would attract his prey, "Well and good, and a fine precept it is! I shall be grateful to learn it well in the coming days. As a leader among my people, I should be grateful for you to come aboard and teach me some of the finer points before I begin in earnest. I perceive that you are a master."

"I shall concede to teach the ignorant Maraldian captain, only as a diversion from my current boredom," mocked the Freemen captain. "I shall board you at my leisure."

"If it pleases you, make haste and bring your officers as well. My own officers are eager to learn and I have many barrels of ale in need of a reason to be emptied!" Gourace embellished the lure and it had its desired effect as the eavesdropping Freemen officers began to argue among themselves which would be allowed to accompany their captain.

As the six top ranking Freemen officers boarded the Maraldian vessel at the fore, 100 Maraldians readied to board the eastern most Freemen ship at the aft.

"Welcome aboard!" Gourace played the gracious host, directing the visiting Freemen to a middeck cabin where plenty of ale was already poured into frothy headed mugs.

"What is that raucous?" inquired the Freemen captain, commenting on the staged party in the adjoining room, intended to create enough noise to mask any shouting or impellor fire from the Freemen vessel which would soon be under siege.

"It is only the revelry of our people glad to be set free from the bondage of Maraldian fetters," Gourace played out the ruse in full. "Please drink your fill and introduce us to the ways of Freeland!"

The Freemen officers were glad enough to relax, drink, and regale the playacting Maraldians with tales of Freeland.

On the far eastern aft of the Freemen ship, a single Maraldian officer dressed as a Freemen scaled the ship's hull with rope and hook and dropped onto the deck.

"Donem's orders," the disguised Maraldian approached the first Freemen he saw, "open the aft hold and prepare to receive Donem and his dignitaries."

"Who are you?" the incredulous Freemen spat back.

"You shall know soon enough if you do not get that hold open in time for Donem's arrival.

"Our captain is away, he said nothing about a visit from Donem," the surprised Freemen sailor replied.

"So your captain is derelict in his duty and you think it wise to do the same? I shall remember you when Donem inquires who is to be put in chains," the Maraldian officer threatened. "I shall open the hold myself."

"No need, no need. I'm about Donem's business, that's for sure," the intimidated Freemen sailor spoke as he hurried off to open the hold.

Back on the Maraldian vessel, the ale was having its desired effect, as the Freemen officers loudly boasted of their exploits while the Maraldians laughed at every insipid joke.

As the entrance platform to the Freemen hold was readied on the side of the ship, five Maraldian lifeboats of 20 men each edged around the aft.

"What is the meaning of …," the Freemen sailor's words were choked out by the Maraldian imposter as he spied the approaching lifeboats, and a blow to the back of the head insured that the Freemen would not be ready to fight any time soon.

"Welcome aboard!" the imposter helped his comrades enter the Freemen vessel.

"Look at all these weapons!" gushed an excited Maraldian sailor as he lay eyes on the contents of the Freemen ship.

"What's going on here?" shouted another Freemen sailor who had just then descended the stairway into the open hold. He did not wait for a reply.

"Treason! Every man to arms!" the Freemen sailor rallied his comrades. The fight was on.

According to plan, Maraldian teams of two and three quickly spread throughout the Freemen vessel. There was shouting and wrestling in every corridor but few impellor shots were fired and no one on either side suffered more than a broken arm or jaw. The surprised and leaderless Freemen were quickly overwhelmed by the numerous and motivated Maraldians fighting for the lives of their women and children.

The situation for Barve on the western end of the harbor had not been quite so successful as for Gourace on the eastern end and a dozen Maraldian sailors lost their lives in the overthrow. In the end, however, both ships were taken and the top Freemen officers were captive in the Maraldian brigs.

At the pier itself another story was unfolding. As the noise of the tumult in the ships to the east and west became obvious, Donem called in reinforcements directly from the city.

"Men of Ichabod! Our common enemy brings revolt upon us even at our own door! Come now and crush the prize jewel of the Northern King once and for all!" Donem's voice betrayed a hint of panic as he shouted over the rail into the city hole.

However, a successful plea it was as thousands of impellor welding Freemen crawled out of their pit ready to strike a blow at anything with the smell of the north wind upon it.

"Back into the ship, Darrsce, you and your family. The game is over and it is time to flee. I will collect as many of our people who have already disembarked. See, the captured Freemen ships raise sails for a run to open water. Now go," Ravol took charge as Darrsce with his wife and son stood on the pier.

"Not so fast, son," the face of Darrsce's father was as gray as the ground of Ichabod. He pointed a loaded impellor at Darrsce's wife.

"You have wasted your life and I will not let you waste the life of my grandson. He will inherit the wealth of Freeland even if I have to kill you to insure it," said his father, the most he had spoken to Darrsce in years.

"A single Maraldian sunset is worth more than all the wealth of this dungeon hole," Darrsce spoke what he knew would engender ridicule.

PANG! The impellor rang out and Darrsce's wife screamed, falling to the ground bleeding.

In an instant Ravol was on the old man, "Darrsce, take her and your son into the ship and hoist sail at once!"

PANG! Again the impellor rang out as Ravol wrestled on the pier while Darrsce fled with his bleeding wife and terrified son. In a moment the gangplank was raised and the ship weighing anchor.

"You are no match for me, young captain," Darrsce's father taunted, his putrid breath in the face of Ravol. "The power of Freeland is in my bones."

Indeed, Ravol was astonished that such an old man could fight like a youth, and they wrestled until both of them tumbled off the pier and into the water. Splash!

Donem's attention was drawn to the noisy conflict as he returned from the city and he ran toward the end of the pier where it continued.

"Darrsce! You choose a watery grave over the delights of Freeland! I thought you more intelligent than that!" Donem shouted and insulted as he ran.

Nearing the site of the splashing, Donem recognized the combatants. Ravol was finally subduing his foe, holding his head under water as Donem approached.

"I believe it is best for me if you are eliminated," Donem fired his impellor and watched Ravol slump in the water as Darrsce's father gasped for air.

"Sink them where they stand," Donem now turned his attention to the approaching hoard, directing them to fire at will into the hulls of the fleeing ships.

As that gruesome army approached the pier, a sudden north wind gusted over the harbor and pulled at the sails of the bobbing ships. All the captains saw their chance and strained to steer their vessels toward the harbor opening where the two captured Freemen ships where already leading the way. Even the third Freemen ship which stood guard at the mouth of the harbor was blown clear of the harbor entrance, opening a way of escape from the mob now firing indiscriminately from the shore. The weapons wounded a handful of ships but all remained seaworthy until out of impellor range.

"Do not add to me grief upon grief, open your eyes!" Darrsce pleaded with his wounded wife as the ships moved beyond the range of Donem's brood.

Fortunately, Darrsce's father was a novice with the impellor and only succeeded in grazing her shoulder. But the Maraldians were nowhere near free from danger. In fact, the conflict had only just begun.

The ensuing battle with the approaching Freemen ships lasted two full days as the fleeing ships attempted to warn the approaching Maraldian vessels, while at the same time engaging the enraged Freemen in a lopsided sea battle. A third of the newly warned Maraldian vessels chose to continue on to Freeland in spite of the warning and were escorted along unimpeded by the Freemen, while the rest turned about and bought for themselves a fight. In the chaos, the Maraldians were somehow able to commandeer five more Freemen vessels stocked with weapons and use them to provide a measure of cover for the fleeing ships. Yet in the end more than 180,000 of the Maraldians went down to the depths. Young and old, mothers and children, men of courage and those without; the swirling waters dealt with all impartially. Never had the ocean seen such sorrow, never had the sea swallowed so much life. However, it was said by some who escaped that in the midst of the carnage they heard afresh the song of Selah, and there are those now in the Northern Kingdom who attest to it.

Only 23 ships carrying about 15,000 souls, Darrsce and his family being among them, escaped the grasp of the Freemen.

As the small wounded fleet put several days between them and the last sea battle, the sun grew brighter and higher as they exited the realm of twilight. A new breeze began to blow, speeding them back to Maraldia.

Selah, Skud and Noble had just pulled themselves over the last rock outcropping of the day and were ready to make camp. They had been climbing for three months and the vistas only increased in splendor with every step. Enormous canyons roaring with 100 waterfalls, broad meadows flooded in wildflower color and thousands of animals. Villages tucked into forests of gigantic trees, white sandy beaches along crystal clear mountain lakes as wide as an ocean, and cities with buildings of sapphire met them at every turn.

"Do you think we are high enough yet?" Selah asked Noble, deferring to him as the more experienced explorer, "Rivoas said that if we reached the third tier above the Great Temple we would be able to see Maraldia on a clear day."

Something within her wanted to see the place again even if it was so very far away. Their remarkable vision continued to improve the longer they stayed in the Northern Kingdom and especially the higher they climbed.

"We'd have to be pretty high to see over the Tolis but I would guess that we are high enough now, only we are on the wrong side of the ridge to see in the correct direction. It's probably another 15 minutes to the other side. Do you think you have it in you?" Noble playfully insinuated inferior abilities.

"I believe I have a step or two more in me," she acknowledged his little barb with a smile. "Skud, how about you?"

"I'm ready to go up three more tiers but I'll settle for the other side of that ridge," Skud replied and took the lead.

Skud, Selah, and Noble explore the Northern Kingdom

While hiking they reminisced about the old days in Maraldia. There were so many things there that pointed to this place, so many little things that seem obvious now but they were too dull to see or understand it. They talked about how blind they were and about how if they had the vision they enjoy now back in Maraldia they would be able to see these very mountains. As it was, they could not even see the Tolis which was practically on top of them. They talked about the narrow hole and the exploding meteor. They talked about how far Rivoas had to come to bring them back and why he would even bother to do it.

Skud was the first one to crest the ridge.

"Well Selah, there is your fair Maraldia. I can see the outer wall and the glistening of the Elif in the sun. You can't see the half of the city nearest the Tolis because of the angle we're at but I can just make out the square," Skud teased them with details knowing it would make them hike a little faster.

Selah was next to crest.

"Oh my! Ooooh my!" Selah was so full of emotion she covered her mouth and welled up with tears.

Noble crested last.

"Yes yes, isn't that a sight! But what are those dots about 40 stanion from shore?" Noble questioned.

"Those are ships! Freemen ships! One, two...... I count 23 Freemen ships!" Skud, whose vision was now the best of any exclaimed. "But they fly the Maraldian flag. I cannot see the color but I can tell by the shape!"

"We must go down immediately and tell Rivoas!" Selah nearly shouted, excitedly making her way with the others quickly behind.

But Rivoas already knew.

The End

Name Glossary

Bagawind = Bag of wind
Barve = Brave
Ceresin = Sincere
Darrsce = Scarred
Donem = Demon
Elif = Life
Gourace = Courage
Jojus = An old friend of the author's son
Keeres = Seeker
Kwea = Weak
Lered = Elder
Locenes = <u>Lo</u>ve Pea<u>ce</u> Kind<u>ness</u>
Maraldia = <u>Mar</u>ion and Don<u>ald</u>, parents of the author
Noble = Noble, as in personal character
Ravol = Valor
Rivoas = Savior
Rohon = Honor
Sapsion = Passion
Sardis = A biblical city in ancient Turkey that sounds like a girl's name
Selah = A musical annotation from the Psalms
Skud = Just a fun bully name
Stohl = Sloth
Tolis = <u>Tol</u>kien and Lew<u>is</u>, 2 of the author's favorite authors
Torund = Rotund
Turneur = Nurture
Velcer = Clever

14889627R00103

Made in the USA
Charleston, SC
06 October 2012